Also

Sioux Sunrise
Paint the Hills Red
Ghosts Around the Campfire

The Lockes
Last Will
Medicine Wheel

The Law Wranglers
Deal with the Devil
Mouth of Hell (forthcoming)

The Coyote Saga
Night of the Coyote
Return of the Coyote (forthcoming)

DEAL WITH THE DEVIL

The Law Wranglers

a novel by

RON SCHWAB

Poor Coyote Press
An imprint of Leafcutter Publishing Group

Deal with the Devil

by Ron Schwab

Poor Coyote Press
PO Box 6105
Omaha, NE 68106
www.PoorCoyotePress.com

Cover Art: "The Parley" by Frederic Remington

ISBN: 1-943421-16-1
ISBN-13: 978-1-943421-16-9

Deal with the Devil

The Law Wranglers

1

THE INSTANT DANNA'S eyes opened, she sensed someone was in her bedroom. Her body, naked beneath damp, clinging sheets, tensed. She could see nothing in the pitch blackness of the room. She heard no movement. But she could feel his presence. And smell it. The unmistakable, pungent odor of stale sweat and horse dung.

She lay there, motionless and silent, her heart hammering in her chest, listening, waiting, while her mind grasped frantically for a way to escape the danger she knew lurked in the still room. Who was it? A thief? Perhaps he would leave if she feigned sleep. Or did he know she was awake? How had he gotten in? She had locked her doors. Of course, the window latches had seen better days. Damn, the Derringer was still at the gunsmith's. Did she dare try to work her hand beneath her pillow to the lock-back pocket dagger secreted there? No, not yet.

Then she heard movement. The floor creaked. Two tentative steps, perhaps five feet from her bedside. She turned her head slightly, her eyes searching from beneath half-closed lids as they adjusted to the darkness. Then she saw the shadowy, hulking form with a massive chest and shoulders.

"Stay put," came a raspy voice. "You ain't going no place." He stepped toward the bed, yanked away the sheet, and flung it on the floor. She was cornered like a rabbit in a mountain cat's lair. There was no chance to get past the man, and the opposite side of the bed was flush to the wall.

She looked up at the man who towered over her with a leering, broken-toothed smile on his scraggly bearded face. His eyes, puffy and bulging, were illuminated by an eerie band of moonlight that streaked through the curtained window and reminded her of a desert Gila monster's. She tried not to flinch as they surveyed her body with obvious delight.

"Who are you? What do you want?" she demanded, the firmness in her voice belying the icy fear that chilled her spine.

The man grinned back. "A friend of yours asked me to pay you a call . . . a friend that don't take to law wranglers . . . especially nosey female ones." He shook his head slowly back and forth. "I'll be goddamned if I ever seen a lawyer the likes of you. No, ma'am, I sure ain't."

"McKenna sent you," she said, her voice a near whisper.

"I ain't sayin', missy. Don't know that it matters much to you."

He was neither a thief nor a rapist. He had come to her room to kill. Gripped by sudden panic, she leaped up and tried to slip around him, but his fist drove into her cheekbone like a sledge and sent her reeling and dazed back onto the bed. She opened her mouth to scream, but his rough hand clamped over her lips, squeezing, twisting, until she thought her jaw would snap.

"Keep your mouth shut, lady. Think about it. It's late: nobody's going to hear you. Even if they do, nobody's gonna pay a screechin' woman no mind. Figure some whore's just gettin' more than she bargained for. And my compadre's waiting out front. A lot of good folks will be feeding worms if they come snooping. We wouldn't want that, now, would we?"

He was right. It would do her no good to scream. She would only hasten her execution. Time. She needed time. Maybe something would happen; perhaps she could make something happen. She relaxed and lay limp and submissive on the mattress. The man's grip eased. She stood five feet ten inches and was lithe and strong, but this was a big man.

"We understand each other, don't we lawyer lady? You're buying time and I'm bargaining to get me a bonus. Now, I'm going to let loose and you just lay there nice and quiet while I tend to the niceties." He released his grip on her mouth and straightened up.

She gasped for breath, watching him as he unbuckled his gun belt and dropped it on the floor next to the bed. If she could somehow outmaneuver him and get to his six-gun.

"Been a coon's age since I had me some white meat, bitch," the man chortled. "I always got the hankering for it, though."

As he bent over to take off his boots, Danna's hand inched under her pillow, her fingers groping until they closed on the cold pearl handle of the Sheffield folding knife. She worked at the blade, cursing at her clumsiness as she tried to pry it open. Finally, it pulled free from its handle, and she straightened the blade.

She knew that the slender seven-inch blade, so delicate and ornate in appearance, was razor-sharp and deadly, for she had carefully honed it herself. The knife was her only chance, and a feeble one at that, for this was a strong man, one who had likely killed before and could easily turn her own weapon on her. Her grip tightened on the hilt of the knife as the man clumsily shed his trousers. He dropped onto the bed and suddenly grasped her crotch, digging at it with jagged fingernails. She gasped with pain but gritted her teeth and did not pull away, opting for passivity for the moment. He pressed his dry, cracked lips roughly against her mouth, but she was a limp ragdoll, neither responding nor resisting. The attacker pulled back his head, glaring into her eyes, breathing heavily, blowing his rancid breath onto her face.

"What the hell's the matter with you, woman?" he said, his voice husky. "You ain't got no spunk at all." When she did not reply, he said, "All right, have it your way. We'll get this done and I'll be about my business."

He moved on top of her, his heavy body nearly crushing her breathless. She could feel his hard maleness probing against her as he tried to wedge between her resisting thighs.

"Leastways, you ain't dead," he said, "yet."

She clamped her thighs, trying now to squirm her hips out from under him, but his breathing was labored and excited, and he drove himself against her with a force that revealed his urgency. The time was right. His mind was consumed by a single thought.

"Bitch. Goddamn bitch," he croaked. He raised up, slapping her harshly several times before striking her across the bridge of the nose with his fist. She moaned, tears glazing her eyes from the searing pain that ripped through her skull. She clenched her teeth against her lower lip until blood came, struggling against the panic that was trying to overtake her.

"Now, hump," he commanded, "or I'll beat your face to a bloody pulp."

Brutally, he jerked her legs apart and collapsed on top of her. He raised his buttocks in readiness to plunge into her just as her hand slipped from beneath the pillow and arced downward, driving the narrow, pointed blade of the dagger hilt-deep into his thickly muscled shoulder. She drew it back as he yelped in pain and reared up to his knees.

"Oh, Jesus," he groaned, just before she scrambled out from under him and thrust the blade beneath his rib cage. "Oh, no," he sobbed. "Oh, damn, no." He moaned in agony as one hand clutched his wounded belly and the other latched onto the wrist of her weaponless hand, wrenching it sharply and yanking her toward him.

"I'll kill you. I'll—" His words were cut off by his own hysterical screams as Danna's dagger stabbed and slashed at his groin. He tumbled backward off the bed. Like a cat, she leaped after him, slicing at his back while he struggled to his feet, sobbing and cursing alternately as he stumbled to the door.

She caught sight of the door opening just a crack. She had forgotten: the man outside. Where had the bastard left his damn six-gun? She bent over, rummaging through the boots and trousers on the floor until her hand came upon the cold butt of the pistol. She drew it from the holster and whirled toward the door. Crouching by the side of the bed, she watched as her attacker reached the door and pulled it open. In the doorway stood a stocky gunman whose menacing form was outlined perfectly against the moonlit outer office.

"Blackie, what the hell's going on?" yelled the startled gunman, his eyes darting about the room, his pistol poised to fire. The big man—Blackie—was doubled over in pain.

"I'm hurt," he choked. "Hurt bad. Kill the bitch, then get me out of here." Blackie pushed past the gunman and disappeared into the law office.

The stocky man peered into the room and stepped cautiously

through the doorway. She had the advantage now. His eyes were foreign to the darkness. She raised the six-gun, aimed, and squeezed the trigger. Her first bullet tore into the gunman's throat; before he sunk to the floor, the second slammed dead center into his chest. She heard the front door open and close. She waited until she heard the pounding of a horse's hooves racing away and then tossed the smoking pistol onto the bed. She moved to the doorway, where she shoved the dead man's obstructing leg into the office, closed the door, and locked it.

Ignoring the commotion outside, she found a lucifer and lit the oil lamp. Using the last of the water in the porcelain pitcher on the table, she washed and cleansed herself as best she could, leaving the water in the basin a dark crimson before she was finished. Only then was she aware of the relentless pain that wracked her nose and cheekbone. She picked up her knife from where she had dropped it before taking up the attacker's gun. Handling it with almost reverent tenderness, she cleaned the blade carefully before folding it back into its handle.

She glanced at the sheets of her bed; they looked like someone had tossed a bucket of bright red paint on them. But it was not paint that splotched the white sheets. A small bloodied object next to the pistol caught her eye. She stepped over to the bed. She shivered involuntarily. Blackie's finger, perhaps? She picked up the pistol and poked tentatively at the object. The bile rose up in her throat as she realized Blackie had departed absent the head of his penis.

She turned away from the bed, hearing for the first time the pounding on her door. "Danna? You all right in there?" asked a man with traces of a southern drawl.

She recognized the voice of Doc Middleton from down the

street. "Yes, I'm fine," she said. "I'll be with you in a moment."

She brushed back the thick, strawberry-blonde hair that cascaded over her shoulders, trying to pat it into place. Then she slipped into her undergarments and a gingham dress and straightened her skirt before stepping toward the door. There was work to be done; she had to report this to the federal marshal. And it was time to associate with another lawyer on this case.

2

JOSH RIVERS AWOKE at the sound of the soft, timid rapping on the bedroom door. He rolled over on his side and placed a lazy hand on the smooth round hip of the tawny-skinned woman who slumbered beside him. The sight of her there, vulnerable, inviting in her nakedness, aroused him again and he scooted closer, slipping his hand up her side and cupping her firm, full breast. She responded to his touch and turned to face him, her black velvety eyes opening drowsily. She smiled warmly. "My stallion," she purred. "My *magnifico* stallion." She opened her arms to receive him when the knocking came at the door again, this time louder, but still hesitant.

"Señorita Hidalgo, are you in there?" came the thickly accented voice of a young Mexican woman.

"Of course, Rosa," snapped Constanza Hidalgo, her dark eyes flashing angrily. "Where else would I be? How dare you bother me when I am taking my siesta? Go away."

"But señorita . . . I have a message from the office of señor Rivers. The boy said it was very important that I should deliver it to you *instante*."

Constanza slipped out of Josh's grasp and sat up. Her lips formed a little pout and she glared down at Josh. "It must be for you," she said.

Josh grinned sheepishly. "That's possible."

"Your office would not send a message to me. Joshua, how did they know?"

Josh reached for her. "Who cares? Forget the message. Tell her to come back later."

She eluded him, sprang from the bed, and scurried around the room, trying to retrieve her scattered garments, as Josh propped himself up on one elbow and watched with an amused smile, savoring the gazelle-like movement of her lithe body. There were none more beautiful than Constanza in all of Santa Fe, he thought. None more passionate.

“Señorita?” came the voice again from outside the door.

"*Un momento.*" She abandoned her search and snapped up the pink satin sheet that had been tossed off the bed during the heat forged from the combined effects of the early afternoon sun and their fervent lovemaking. She wrapped it around her like a sarong and took a step toward the door before she turned and shot him a look of disgust. "You cannot sit there like that," she said.

"Like what?"

"You are naked. She will see you. Rosa would die. Besides, I do not want her to know."

"She knows."

"No. Unless she sees you, she only guesses. Quickly. On the floor . . . behind the bed."

He grabbed the pillow and propped it over his lap. "There, I'm covered." But he saw she was in no mood to be teased and he shrugged in resignation. "All right, the floor. But I feel silly as hell." He disappeared over the far side of the bed.

Constanza, clutching the sheet tight about her, moved to the door and opened it. The plumpish house servant stood wide-eyed in the open doorway.

"I . . . I am sorry, señorita Hidalgo," she said in Spanish. "I did not wish to bother you."

Constanza smiled benignly and replied in her native tongue. "It is all right, Rosa. I was only napping. As you know, I am cross when I am awakened. Please forgive me for being so sharp with you."

"It is all right, señorita. I understand."

"And now, Rosa, the message."

The girl's eyes had been studying the bedroom behind Constanza. "Oh, yes, the message. Here." Rosa handed Constanza the sheet of paper and backed away, smiling nervously.

"Rosa," Constanza said sweetly.

"Yes, señorita?"

"I would prefer that you said nothing to my father about this message. Is that understood?"

"Oh, yes, señorita. Never. There would be no cause to say anything to your father."

Constanza closed the door and walked slowly to the bed. "Just as I thought," she said. "Your name is on it." She flipped the note onto the bed. Josh rose up from his hiding place and reached over and picked up the note.

"How did they know you were here?" Constanza asked.

"I'm a lawyer. My clerk has to know where I can be reached." He unfolded the note and tried to make out the barely legible scrawl of his law clerk: *Levi waiting in your office. Says he needs to see you pronto. Had to talk him out of hunting for you himself. Crabby as hell. Hurry. George*

He crumpled up the note, tossed it on the floor, and moved around the bed toward Constanza who had been watching him intently. "I have to leave soon," he said.

"*Bastardo*," she hissed. "Am I but one of your clients that I must have an appointment?"

They stood beside the bed facing each other. "Don't be angry," he cajoled. "You are dear to me, Constanza. More precious than all the gold in these mountains. I treasure my time with you, but I have my work. Please try to understand." He saw her eyes soften and he knew how it would end. She wanted him as badly as he wanted her. That was the way it should be, and that was the bond between them.

He took her in his arms and pressed his lips to hers as the silky sheet slithered down the length of her slender body and fell in a heap at her feet.

3

JOSH STROLLED LEISURELY across the plaza toward his office which was housed in one of the single-story plastered, adobe brick buildings that lined the streets of Santa Fe's commercial center. He was dressed impeccably in a low-crowned hat and gabardine suit that nearly matched the rust-brown color of his thick, wiry hair. He was tall, well over six feet, with one of those lean, loose frames that seemed to mold, like pliant wax, to whatever garment adorned it at the time. He had a penchant for fine clothes, and he indulged it when fees were good.

He wondered what had brought his father the nearly eighty miles down the Santa Fe Trail from the Slash R ranch. The old man could be counted on to show up in the middle of November to hole up for the winter, and at the first sign of spring thaw he always moved out to the ranch with a wagon train of supplies to replenish the warehouses and company trading post on the sprawling ranch. Never had he returned in June.

Josh tipped his hat to a pretty, young Mexican woman who was displaying farm produce with dozens of others of her people in the shade of the portico that rimmed the plaza, and she flashed a warm smile that made him think of Constanza. Damn, she was a woman to while away the hours with. Intelligent and well-read, speaking at least four languages fluently, she was the epitome of refined and genteel Spanish aristocracy. And still, there was a wild, uninhibited, totally physical side to her that incited his lust and sated him in a way no other woman ever had. They were good together. Did he love her, he wondered. Yes, in many ways. But enough to marry her? Not now; not while he still carried Cassie's ghost in his heart. But if he were inclined to marry, Constanza would be a good choice, in more ways than love.

The Hidalgos were a powerful Santa Fe family. Miguel Hidalgo claimed a pure bloodline from Mother Spain. He was Spanish, not Mexican, he repeatedly reminded his fellows in aristocratic Santa Fe circles, and he held one of the largest contiguous land grants in the New Mexico territory. Constanza was his only child and would be an extremely wealthy woman someday. It was too bad, Josh thought, that he didn't give a damn about the stuffy old fart's money. Not that Hidalgo would welcome a gringo son-in-law with open arms . . . especially one with Josh's melting pot heritage.

When Josh stepped into the front room of his comfortable office suite, George Hatter peered up at him over wire-rimmed spectacles with a look of mild exasperation on his cherubic face. "You've been gone three hours, Josh," Hatter chided. "When you left, you said you'd be back within the hour. Your father's been prancing around here like a stud waiting to go service, if you'll pardon the expression. I have been able to get nothing done . . . absolutely nothing."

George was an old woman. He always got plenty done, and Josh readily conceded that he needed a mother hen to look after the office. "Where is he?"

"In your office . . . sitting at your desk the last I saw him."

When Josh walked into his office, he was greeted by the sweet-acrid smell of cigar smoke. Its source was a white-haired man with a leathery, lined face that was baked as brown as an Indian's, who leaned back in the high-backed swivel chair behind Josh's desk with his dusty-booted feet tossed casually over the broad, shiny desktop. Take Levi Rivers out of his faded blue jeans and dirty denim shirt and put him in a tailored suit, and the rangy rancher might be Josh in another forty years when he was pushing seventy. He was his old man's look-alike, or so his brothers always claimed. Perhaps, but their physical resemblance was about all they had in common.

Levi Rivers plucked the cigar from his mouth and exhaled a thick plume of smoke as he scrutinized his son with piercing dark brown eyes that matched Josh's own. "Have a chair," Levi growled, nodding toward one of the leather-upholstered arm chairs in front of the desk.

"You're very kind," Josh said sardonically, as he let himself down into the chair, promising himself that this time he would not lose his temper, no matter what the old man said.

Levi puffed again on his cigar, and then nodded toward the stack of papers on the oak desk. "Looks like you got plenty of work to do."

"I keep busy," Josh replied, noncommittally.

"Nobody ever drowned himself in his own sweat."

"I've heard that somewhere before, Pop."

"Your brother Nate and me, we got to work to make ends meet."

"You work because you want to, Pop; so does Nate. With

twenty thousand acres and cattle to fill it, you don't have to work so hard. You do it because you want to. The ranch is your lifeblood, but it is not mine. I've got my own work."

"Humph," Levi snorted. "Law wrangling ain't real work. I don't see any calluses on your hands. If you got any, they're on your ass. Four boys I sire, and Nate's the only one that's got the gumption to stick it out on the ranch. Rivers Land & Cattle Company . . . the Slash R . . . it's the biggest spread in the north half of New Mexico territory. Big enough for all my sons to make their places there. And what do I get out of my sons? A law wrangler, a banker, and a drifter. I had hopes for your little sister. I thought maybe Tabitha would put a rope around one of the foremen someday. That gal was always one of the best cowhands on the ranch, but like a jackass I let your mother . . . God rest her soul . . . talk me into sending her off to that finishing school in Denver. Then the damn fool gal stays on for college. Goddamn, where'd I go wrong? What next? Women in college. Next they'll want the right to vote."

"They've already got it in Wyoming Territory, Pop."

"Thank God I won't live long enough to see it here."

"Pop, you don't make sense. Look at Tabby. She's smarter than any man I know. And she's got a fine job."

"Like hell. A goddamned writer. She ought to be on the ranch. Some cowboy's wife. She's practically an old maid."

Josh said nothing, letting his father work the fire out of his system. He had endured the old man's rampages before, and he had long since concluded that Levi Rivers's harangues were smoke screens to hide a secret pride that he harbored in his progenies' accomplishments and independent ways.

Levi's eyes suddenly grew distant and filmy with moistness.

"It was Aurelie's fault. That's what I get for marrying a schoolmarm. From the time we had our first born, all she could talk about was education, education, education. And she got her way as usual. Only woman who ever had a ring in my nose. All you kids got educated, all right. Educated right off the Slash R."

Josh knew that any irritation directed in Aurelie Rivers's way was feigned by his father, for she was his one true love. He had never quite recovered from her death under a Comanche war axe some five years back on that spring morning when Josh's own raven-haired Cassandra was raped and mutilated before she suffered the same fate. The Comanche usually stayed away from the mountain valleys, preferring to roam the flatlands of the plains of western Texas and eastern New Mexico, and the Rivers family had lived with an unwarranted sense of security in the more lush valley grasslands, crisscrossed by mountain streams that provided year-round water for their thriving cow herds.

It had been a bright, brisk morning with a glittering sun gilding the Sangre de Cristo Mountains that reached for azure skies to the west of the Slash R home-ranch compound. On that bright, spring morning created by whatever God ruled above for those who relished life, his infant son, Michael Levi Rivers, had disappeared, seemingly from the face of the earth. Josh felt a rare moment of communion with his father, born of their common tragedy. Then he spoke reassurance.

"Come on, Pop. Your brood hasn't turned out so bad. Your eldest is on the ranch, a cattleman, and a damn good businessman to boot. Ham's president of the largest bank in Colorado, and Cal will be back on the ranch sooner or later. His scouting contract with the Army was up last month. And Tabby, she has a real talent for the written word. Journalists sowed the seeds that brought this country into being. You're always ranting about power, Pop. Tell me an institution in this territory that's more powerful than *The Santa Fe New Mexican*. And that paper's publishing Tabby regularly. Tabby will do credit to the Rivers name. You can count on it. As for me, I'm paying my own bills."

Josh winced when Levi snuffed out the cigar on the varnished desktop.

"Looks to me like you're living plenty high on the hog, all right, Joshua. It might be better if you'd stay in your office and take care of your business."

"Sometimes my business takes me out of my office," Josh countered, and as he answered, he wondered why he always felt compelled to respond to his father's charges. He explained himself to no other man.

A wry smile crossed Levi's weathered face. "Only business you've been on today has been monkey business. You got that contented look like my old tomcat always gets after he's partook of one of the females."

Josh flushed slightly before his father's perceptiveness.

The old man continued. "But I'm talking about your taking off for days, maybe weeks at a time."

"It's part of my work, Pop. I handle special problems for people. Besides, George looks after things while I'm gone, and Linda de la Cruz is going to be a fine secretary with more experience. And she's a great help dealing with her people."

"But they ain't lawyers. Santa Fe's the territorial capital, the center of commerce. You'd find more than enough opportunity here without gallivanting all over hell and gone. I ask around when I'm in town. My old pards tell me folks think high of you. I can't see why, but they say you could put a half a dozen lawyers to work."

"Pop, there's no use arguing about it. I'll never convince you big isn't necessarily better; sometimes it's worse. I'll admit I could use some help, and I suppose I'll have to take in another lawyer or two eventually, but I've got an independent streak. Where do you suppose I got that? Anyway, I can't just partner with anybody, but I'm keeping my eyes open for the right man." He clasped his hands behind his neck and stretched his long legs out in front of him. "Now, Pop, you're right, I do have plenty of work to do, and you didn't ride in here all the way from the Slash R to offer me some business advice. You're not making social calls in Santa Fe this time of year, so why don't you just spit it out?"

Levi hoisted his feet off of Josh's desk, straightened up in the chair, and reached into his back trousers pocket and pulled out a crumpled envelope. "I got a case for you," he said. He flipped the envelope across the desk top to Josh. "You can read it later," Levi said. "It's from a lawyer by the name of D. L. Sinclair over at Madison, near the Oklahoma and Texas borders . . . Colorado's just a little north. The lawyer's handling some business for Bill McKenna's sister-in-law, Dawn Rutledge. Bill was the best and longest friend I had on this earth. He was killed a while back. You met him a couple of times when you was still at home. He brought me some prize Durham stock once."

"I remember him. You talked about Bill McKenna all the time when we were growing up. You came west together and were in the same company during the Texas war. Weren't you partners once?"

"Yep, but I guess I wasn't one to partner so good, either. I realized old Bill and me would never see things the same way in business. After I met your ma, I bought a place of my own, so Bill and me split up while we was still friends. We both did good without each other. He built up a big spread near the Dry Cimarron River and Folsom Falls not far from Madison. Guess it goes to show you that there are different ways of getting to the same place."

"What happened to McKenna?"

"Comanche." He paused. "Kwahadi," he added meaningfully. "They killed Bill and burned the home place to the ground. They got away with Bill's daughter, Erin. Whether she's dead or alive, nobody knows for sure."

The old man was feeding him bait. Abducted child. Kwahadi. "What does this have to do with a case for me?" Josh asked, working the letter out of the envelope Levi had handed him.

Levi's eyes narrowed. "Dawn Rutledge is faced with losing the ranch to Bill's brother Oliver. Bill's got to be rolling over in his grave right now. Oliver McKenna's as crooked as a snake in a cactus patch. It won't matter to him none how he gets the ranch, but once he does, he'll sell it and walk away with a bundle of cash to sink into some other scheme of his. That letter will tell you more about it." Levi bit off the tip of a fresh cigar and rolled it contemplatively between his fingertips. "It seems Bill's been gone more than a year now, and I didn't even know. You see, Bill's wife died birthing the girl and Miss Rutledge was his wife's old maid sister. She moved in to raise the girl. I got a notion she took care of Bill, too, if you know what I mean. Anyhow, she recollected hearing Bill talk about me and how I had a son in the law business who had had some dealings with the Comanche. When she told the lawyer about that, he decided to write to me and see if I might be of some help."

"Your friend, McKenna, did he have a will?"

"Nope. Bill never did nothing on paper. That was one reason we parted company. He couldn't read or write except to scrawl his name, but he didn't like folks to know. I guess that's why he never got around to making out a will. That seems to be the cause of Miss Rutledge's trouble. Since she's not Bill's widow, under territorial law, she gets nothing. And she wouldn't have no kick about that if Bill's girl got it. But that bastard, Oliver, he's gone to court to have Erin McKenna declared dead. I don't know Dawn Rutledge too good . . . I only met her a few times . . . but I know that Bill would rather have the devil himself end up with the Circle M than for Oliver to get his filthy paws on it."

"Just what does this Mr. Sinclair want me to do?"

"Well, it seems like Oliver McKenna is starting to play rough. Mr. Sinclair seems to have more than he can handle and would like to hire you to help out."

"There are other lawyers in New Mexico."

"Not many that would know about hunting for a girl among the Comanche," Levi said.

"My record for finding captive children among the Comanche is not enviable, Pop." At those words, it was like a mask of sadness slipped over Levi's face, and Josh thought he saw something akin to desperation in the eyes that bore into his own from across the desk.

"Joshua," Levi pleaded, "your Michael is still alive on the Staked Plains . . . somewhere. I feel it in these old bones of mine. My only grandson's being raised by murdering savages. You can try to find him again, just one more time, and maybe do some other folks a good turn in the course of it."

"Pop, I spent the better part of the first year after Mom and Cassie were killed looking for Michael. I've been out twice since.

A child that small, a war party days away from any village . . . there's hardly any chance that they kept him alive . . . or even tried to. There comes a time to go on. I've put it behind me . . . as much as a man can.”

He could see that the old man knew he was lying. Josh continued. "If I go, it's strictly a professional trip, and that being the case, can this Dawn Rutledge pay my fees? I don't work cheap."

"You'll see in that letter she can handle that part. She's got some money of her own. You're supposed to get in touch with this lawyer if you're interested. Joshua, I'd like for you to take this job. Ride over to Madison as soon as you can, and check things out for yourself. I feel like the Rivers clan owes old Bill that much."

"You just gave me a tongue thrashing for taking off and leaving my practice all the time, and now you're asking me to do just that. It would take me a good week or more to get up to Madison.”

Levi Rivers pushed back the chair and stood up. "Don't pay attention to what I said. I'm just a dowdy old man; too old to suck and too young to die." He limped toward the office door, stopped and turned back to Josh who had not stirred in his chair. "But you do need some help. You need to get bigger."

"Hold up, Pop," Josh said. "Where do you suppose I could get ahold of Cal? If I was going to take this case . . . and I haven't said I would . . . Cal would be mighty valuable to have along."

His face sober, Levi said, "Calvin's in Taos. I already sent word to him . . . said you needed his help. He'll meet you in Madison. He'll be there before you are."

He was whipped. "Pop, I want you to tell me more about Bill McKenna."

"Why don't you meet me at the Exchange about seven? I'll buy you some grub," Levi answered.

4

JOSH STEPPED UP to the bar in the Cowman's Saloon. The bartender, a bald man with an enormous belly and heavy jowls that seemed suited to his porcine eyes, looked Josh over warily. "No pickings here for a gambler, mister," he said in a raspy voice. "The cowhands had their payday last week and won't have any coin to jangle for a spell."

Josh left the bartender with his curiosity. "I'll have a sarsaparilla."

The man's broad brow wrinkled in a disbelieving frown. "Sure, mister."

Josh heard a few snickers in the sparsely occupied barroom, and reflexively, his fingers caressed the soft leather holster that held the Colt Peacemaker at his side. He had surrendered to the parching sun that baked this dusty New Mexico cow town and abandoned his coat in the hotel room, but with his string bow tie and tailored trousers, he supposed he still looked something of a dandy to these people of the Plains. And he had come to blows with barroom bullies more than once over his taste in drink.

The bartender slid the sarsaparilla bottle across the bar. Josh paid the man and took a swig. It was warm, but did not taste bad, and it washed the dust out of his throat. He wanted to find Cal before he called upon Mr. Sinclair and the most likely place to find him in this barely civilized town was a saloon. Josh found whiskey bitter to the taste, and tequila, so popular in much of the Southwest, numbed his brain before it hit his stomach. A fine wine on occasion with a gourmet meal or with an elegant woman —preferably both—and consumed in moderation, more than satisfied his thirst for spirits. He had an aversion to anything that might dull his senses or slow his mind. He believed that his relative temperance gave him an edge, whether in a gunfight or a courtroom or a boudoir.

Not so, Cal. He drank anything, discriminating against no liquor regardless of national origin. And his tolerance seemingly knew no limits. Cal could spend weeks on the trail without a drop of whiskey, but when he rode into town for a week of drinking and womanizing, he guzzled the booze like spring water. Yet, after he had drunk everyone else under the table, he would walk out of the saloon on steady legs and rendezvous with the woman of his choice for a night of frolic. Josh could not imagine Calvin Rivers tumbling dead drunk into some whore's bed and sleeping away the time he had purchased like some cowboys had been known to do.

Josh cast a glance toward the saloon door and took another drink. No, the Rivers clan was an independent bunch. Each of Levi Rivers's sons was making his own way through life, chasing his own dreams, and more often than not, catching them. And it looked like Tabby was going to be of the same mold. She was fiercely proud, undaunted by adversity, and she was likely the smartest of the clan.

How old would she be now? He always lost track of ages. He had to start at the bottom or top of the family, and then he could remember all the others. She had been sixteen when the Comanche hit the once invincible Slash R compound, with its thick adobe walls surrounding the ranch buildings like a fortress. Five years had passed since Tabby had broken free from her Comanche captors and outraced them in a frantic dash for the icy waters of the Canadian River and disappeared into its depths. It was Tabby, after she made her way back to the smoldering rubble of the ranch homestead, who confirmed that tiny Michael had indeed been spared, for a time, at least. But she had escaped the raiders only after some of the Indians in the war party had separated from the main band, taking Michael Rivers with them.

That would make her twenty-one now. But a wise and strong and very mature twenty-one.

Tabby, the baby, the afterthought, was seven years younger than Cal, who at twenty-eight was a year younger than Josh. Hamilton would be nearly thirty-three now; that would make Nate thirty-five. Strange, Josh thought, the siblings rarely saw each other, yet as they followed their separate trails, there was an undeniable sense of family that their parents had somehow built within them, a bond that held them each fast to the other without calling for any surrender of individuality—a bond that had its roots in the Slash R. Had it been planned by Levi and Aurelie, or had it just happened?

"Hey, Sonny," came a slurred, belligerent voice from behind Josh, yanking him from his musings. "You sure that apple juice you're drinkin' ain't a bit strong for you?"

Ignoring the heckler, Josh pressed the soda bottle to his lips again.

"I'm talking to you, dude. Big Frank ain't used to asking questions twice."

This time, Josh turned his head just enough to catch a glimpse of the scraggly oaf who was staggering his way past the tables and chairs and moving in on Josh's right. Josh turned back to the bar. He was a big man, all right, perhaps not as tall as himself, but outweighing him by a good hundred pounds. Shoulders and biceps like huge hams. Big chest, thick and broad as a buffalo bull's. A little soft in the belly, maybe, but there was no way Josh Rivers was going to whip Big Frank in a fair fight.

"I'm waiting, mister," Big Frank said, his voice booming in Josh's ears.

"The sarsaparilla's not too strong," Josh said. "I think I can handle it."

"That a yeller streak I see runnin' down your back, mister?"

A rough hand closed in a vice-like grip on Josh's shoulder and spun him around. Josh saw Big Frank's idiotic yellow-toothed smile for just a second before the man's grimy, whisker-stubble face twisted in agony as Josh's knee drove into his groin with full force. Big Frank doubled over in pain, gasping helplessly for breath, before Josh's fist hammered into the side of his nose. Josh heard the crunch of bone that told him he had broken the man's nose, but taking no chances, he slipped his Peacemaker from its holster, feinted off to the side of the dazed, tottering bully, and slammed the long pistol barrel against Big Frank's temple. The blow felled him like a slain bear, and he collapsed in a heap on the barroom floor. He lay there in the stunned silence of the room, blood streaming in rivulets down the side of his face, spewing from his shattered nose.

Josh's eyes scanned the room, searching the faces of the half dozen or so other men who sat frozen in their chairs. There were no other challengers. He holstered his pistol and turned back once again to the bar. "I'll have another sarsaparilla," he said matter-of-factly to the bartender, whose incredulous eyes betrayed an otherwise impassive face.

Ten minutes passed. The bartender stood behind the bar, unmoving, studying Josh with beady eyes as he downed his second sarsaparilla. His customers remained glued to the chairs at their tables, their eyes fixed on Big Frank who lay on the floor, his head resting in a pool of blood. No one had entered the saloon. No one had left. It was as if they were all waiting for someone or something, but did not know for whom or for what.

Finally, the barroom doors squeaked open, breaking the silence and the tension, and it was as if an inaudible sigh of relief breathed through the room. Josh tossed a glance at the doorway, and his lips spread in a sheepish smile. He acknowledged the newcomer with a nod of his head as the raw-boned man in the fringed deerskin shirt strode toward him.

"Good afternoon, little brother," Josh said as he extended his hand to the man who stood several inches taller than himself. "I figured you'd show up here sooner or later."

Cal Rivers took Josh's hand in a bear-like grip. "Looks like it should have been sooner," he said, sliding up to the bar. "Welcome to Madison."

"I don't suppose I can buy you a drink," Josh said.

"More than one, I hope," said the man with a boyish face, whipping off his round-brimmed Plainsman hat and tossing it on the bar, before brushing the dust out of his shaggy, wheat-straw colored hair.

"Whiskey?" Josh asked.

"A bottle will do fine."

They retired to a table in one corner of the barroom, and while the surly barkeep directed the removal of the still-unconscious Big Frank from the premises, the brothers caught each other up on the happenings during their year's separation. Josh leaned back in his chair and listened with relish as Cal related tales of his half year as a scout for Colonel Ranald Slidell Mackenzie's Fourth Calvary beginning the summer of 1872 and ending after the onset of winter. In some ways, he envied his younger brother. Cal never knew a stranger.

Although the youngest of the four Rivers sons, Cal was the tallest and physically strongest. But in spite of his intimidating size, he was generally affable as a pup. People liked him and even now as he nursed his whiskey bottle and told Josh stories, the truth of which had to be questioned by any intelligent man, it was hard as hell not to believe him when he looked at you from beneath thick blond eyebrows with those clear-blue, sincere eyes.

But Josh had an impatience for small talk. His interest quickly waned to boredom and during one of Cal's stories of a Comanche chase, he found his opening. "Speaking of Comanche, Cal," Josh said, "I don't know how much Pop wrote you, but that's why you're here."

"Pop didn't tell me anything. I got the telegram in Taos. In a few days I was going to ride down to Fort Clark and sign on to scout for Mackenzie's fall campaign. All the telegram said was that you needed help and I was to get to Madison *pronto*. Pop's never asked me for anything unless he had a good cause. So here I am. But what's this about Comanche? I thought I was getting a vacation from those devils."

Josh related the story as he had received it from the lawyer's letter. "I'll know more after I visit with Mr. Sinclair. Any idea where I might find his office?"

"Yep. I saw the sign over the door. I remember because it was fresh-painted. Right here on Main Street. Turn to the left when you go out the door, about two blocks down on this side of the street."

"Do you want to go with me?" Josh asked.

"Nope. About the least interesting thing I can think of to do right now is to listen to two law wranglers palaver. From what you say, I'd better enjoy my whiskey while I got the chance." He winked and grinned broadly. "I met a lady friend when I rode in here a few days back. I'll go calling after a bit. I'll find you at the hotel later. They've got a decent café there. You can buy me supper. But Josh, there's something you ought to know."

"What's that?"

"That jasper you kicked the hell out of . . . Big Frank Crenshaw . . . he's got a reputation for being one mean bastard."

"You aren't telling me anything new. I could see that on his ugly face."

"Yeah, but there's something else. He works for Oliver McKenna."

Josh rubbed the back of his neck thoughtfully. "I didn't exactly lay the groundwork for congenial negotiations, did I?"

5

JOSH HAD NO trouble finding D. L. Sinclair's office. It was a narrow, one-floor building with a weathered board front sandwiched in between two comparatively imposing structures, one a general store and the other an establishment with a huge sign stretching across the length of the building that identified it as Withers Furniture and Undertaking. A lawyer could do worse than set up shop next to an undertaker, Josh thought. It sure couldn't hurt the probate business any, but was probably not quite what the old man called a “license to steal” situation.

In sharp contrast to the signs of the adjoining buildings, the lawyer's shingle was freshly painted in sharp black script on a shiny white board. It struck Josh that the displayer of the sign, the class and professionalism of which seemed so out of place on the ramshackle building front, would be a person of considerable professional pride. He paused a moment, admiring the sign. The words were simple: D. L. Sinclair, Lawyer. Pride without pretense. Josh had always had an instinctive, albeit illogical, suspicion of those lawyers who held themselves out as "attorneys and counselors" or "counselors at law." He looked upon those who called themselves "attorneys" or "attorneys at law" with less disdain. He considered himself a lawyer and preferred to deal with others who labeled themselves thus.

There was no one to greet him when he walked into the lawyer's office, and he guessed that the occupant was gone for the moment on some errand. He tossed his hat on the hall tree in one corner and began to slowly pace the room. After days in the saddle, none of the three hard oak chairs that lined the front wall were inviting.

The room was austere, sparsely furnished with a single roll top desk at one side wall and a low-backed swivel chair beside it. There was a book case stuffed with statute books and some tattered hornbooks, and a warped, wood filing cabinet. He walked over to the desk and examined the two framed documents that hung on the wall above it, the larger of the two proclaiming that the holder of the certificate was duly admitted to practice in the Federal District Court of the Territory of New Mexico. The other evidenced a bachelor of law degree issued by the University of Virginia. It was a rarity on the frontier: a practicing lawyer who was a graduate of a recognizable school. Josh himself had received his degree at the Hastings College of Law in San Francisco, but the vast majority of his colleagues had been admitted to the bar after reading the law or clerking in an established office for some years prior to taking the bar examination. Many were excellent lawyers; others were inept. But the same could be said of lawyers who held degrees from Harvard and Yale.

However, it was not the diploma that surprised him so much, as it was the name of the grantee of the law degree.

The office door opened, and a young woman with a folder of legal papers tucked under one arm stepped in. She held him speechless for a moment as she looked at him with an uncertain smile on her fair, Nordic face. She wore a high-necked dress, pale blue in color that complimented her glittering sapphire-blue eyes. Her reddish-gold hair was swept back and tied with a blue satin ribbon before it cascaded over her shoulder to the middle of her back. She was a stunning woman, Josh thought, unexplainably trying to compare her to Constanza. The woman was noticeably taller than the dark-haired Spanish beauty but not as fine-boned. No, he could not compare the two. It would be like comparing a ruby to an emerald. A matter of taste or preference, perhaps depending upon the day, the hour, the moment.

Then he became aware of the prolonged silence they had shared, and it was suddenly awkward. As if on cue, she stepped toward him with her slender hand outstretched. "I'm Danna Sinclair," she said, her voice friendly, yet businesslike. "May I help you?"

He accepted her hand, a bit surprised at the firmness of her handshake. "Yes, ma'am, I take it you're D. L. Sinclair." He wished he could take back the words the moment he uttered them. He had read the name on the diploma and bar certificate. For some reason, though, this damn woman had unnerved and flustered him, and he was not familiar with that feeling.

"Yes, the D. L. stands for Danna Lee. I have to admit that I use my initials for somewhat deceptive purposes. I hope you're not too disappointed, Mr.—"

"I'm sorry, ma'am. My name's Josh Rivers. You wrote to my father about the McKenna case."

"Yes, of course," she said. "I'm so glad you've come. I never received a response from your father so I didn't know whether to expect you." She moved to the swivel chair next to her desk.

"Won't you pull up a chair?" she said, before nodding toward the closed door at the rear of the room. "I do have a small private office, but I rarely use it. It has no desk, just two chairs in a bare room. My living quarters are behind that. It's a fair assumption that we won't be interrupted. I have no clerk or secretary, and clients don't exactly beat a path to my door."

Josh guessed she could be no more than twenty-five years old. "It takes time to build a practice," he said. "How long have you been here?"

"A little more than a year. Miss Rutledge was my first client. I draft a few wills and handle a real estate transaction on occasion, but it is very slow."

"Madison looks like a growing town," Josh said. "I noticed a lot of building activity when I rode into town,"

"Unfortunately, it's mostly owned by Oliver McKenna. The only future here seems to be in representing him, so I suspect I'll be moving soon."

"Where to?"

"I've considered Fort Worth, but women aren't admitted to the Texas Bar yet. That would keep me from practicing in the state courts, and I'm not certain I could earn a living in the federal courts alone. That isn't a problem in a territory like New Mexico, though, where there isn't a state bar."

"Why did you choose Madison in the first place?"

"I was raised on a ranch in south Texas and I know the cattle business forward and backward. I wanted to grow with the town, if I didn't starve out first." She smiled again. It was an easy, contagious smile. "Don't misunderstand me, Mr. Rivers. I have no chips on my shoulder. I love what I'm doing and am grateful to be doing it. But I wouldn't object to doing more of it. Now, I suggest we get down to business. I assume you wouldn't be here unless you were interested in working with me on the case."

"Yes," he agreed, "but I have a feeling it wasn't my services as a lawyer that you were soliciting. Your letter sounded like you were more interested in hiring me to ransom or steal Erin McKenna back from the Comanche. My brother Cal met me here. He has some experience scouting with the Army. He'll help if we take on the job. But I should warn you, I've made such a search before, with more at stake than a fee in it, and I'd say that the odds are very much against finding the girl."

Sadness clouded her eyes and they seemed to turn a darker blue. "Miss Rutledge told me of your loss, Mr. Rivers. I'm truly sorry. I know that our chances are slim at best, but Erin McKenna's more woman than girl. She is nearly eighteen years old. She has fiery red hair, and I'm told she is a very beautiful young lady. She should be quite identifiable."

"That should help," Josh said. "But she's probably some buck's third or fourth wife by now. That will make it harder to get her released, even if we can talk to the Comanche without losing our scalps."

"I'm not comfortable with this, Mr. Rivers, asking a man to risk his life for people he does not even know."

"Lawyers represent people, Miss Sinclair. I'm just a little unorthodox in my representation. Most of my services are rendered outside the courtroom. Besides, this is a personal favor to my father."

Her eyes twinkled. "There is a fee at the end of the rainbow, Mr. Rivers. If we win, I'll split my fees with you. Equal shares, share and share alike."

"And if we lose?"

"The same arrangement. Share and share alike. Unfortunately, fifty percent of nothing is nothing."

"I'm not fond of contingent fees. Just what kind of fee would we be dividing if we win?"

"Three thousand dollars. Dawn Rutledge expects that it will be paid out of Erin's inheritance, but she has signed an agreement backing payment from her own funds, if necessary."

"It's that important to her?"

"You'll find that she is a woman of great principle. She has nothing to gain financially from her efforts. But she raised Erin from a baby; she is more the young woman's mother than aunt."

"Half of three thousand dollars does make it more interesting," Josh said.

"I thought you might see it that way. Why don't I arrange for us to meet with Miss Rutledge in the morning to discuss the details?"

"You seem rather confident that I'll take the case."

"You haven't said no. Besides, you don't strike me as the kind of man who could resist a challenge of this sort. And I doubt you came this far to pass the time of day."

Their eyes locked. He liked this woman, and he sensed a rapport between them, a chemistry that might work very well. Yet he was wary of the feeling. He was reluctant to trust anyone, at least anyone other than blood kin, the way his instincts might lead him to trust Danna Lee Sinclair.

"You've hired yourself an associate, Miss Sinclair."

"I'm glad," Danna replied. "I think we'll make a good team. Since we're going to be associates for a time, I hope you'll call me Danna."

He nodded assent. "I'm Josh."

"Josh," she said, opening one of the files she had placed on the desk when she came into the office. "I know very little about Comanche. Where will you look for Erin McKenna? How long will you be gone?"

"I imagine we'll head for the Staked Plains, but I'll let Cal call the shots. He'll scare up the Kwahadi, but that doesn't mean we'll find the young lady. White captives have a way of disappearing. Some are taken into the tribe; others are traded to the Comanchero or other bands. A young woman that age might end up in a Mexican bordello. Or she could be some man's woman until he tires of her and kills her. If she made too much trouble, she may have been killed and scalped by a Comanche warrior before they ever reached the main band. There's a very good chance that we'll never know what became of Erin McKenna. It's a long shot. How much time do we have?"

"I can give you two months at the most." He rubbed his chin thoughtfully but did not reply. Danna continued. "Oliver McKenna was successful in getting himself appointed administrator of William McKenna's estate based on priority as next of kin. He's filed a petition with the Federal District Court asking that Erin be declared legally dead and for a final determination of William McKenna's heirs. He has an impressive array of witnesses who will testify that there is virtually no chance that Erin is alive. One man, who claims to be a former Indian scout, even brought in some poor soul's skeletal remains and insists that they are Erin's. He also produced a turquoise ring found with the remains that that had the initials 'EM' engraved on it. Erin's aunt insists the young woman owned no such ring. I suspect this piece of evidence was manufactured."

"How solid is the man's testimony?"

"He states he recovered the remains from a Comanche who had taken Erin as his wife. His testimony is hearsay, of course, totally without proper evidentiary foundation, but that is not likely to matter a great deal. I suppose I'm being disrespectful of the Court, but Judge Andrew Robinson of our circuit court would rule that horse shit was the excrement of a jack rabbit if his friend, Peter Dimona, told him it was so."

"Peter Dimona?"

"Mr. Dimona is a reincarnation of Shakespeare's Shylock . . . the kind of lawyer who consigns our profession to a perpetual state of public disrepute. Oliver McKenna is Dimona's sole client, and he serves his master well. What was it Cornelius Vanderbilt said? 'What do I care about the law? Ain't I got the power?' Dimona always brings that quote to mind. Judge Robinson has set Dimona's petition for hearing in Santa Fe on the fifteenth of August. He said he won't consider any further motions for continuances. If we can't produce some tangible evidence that Erin McKenna is still alive by that time, it's all over. If Judge Robinson rules against us, I can appeal, of course, but chances of success would be very poor, and eventually we would still be faced with producing a live Erin McKenna."

"So we have less than two months. Cal and I had better ride out by the day after tomorrow. I want to know more about Oliver McKenna before we go. And I need to spend some time with Cal working out our plans."

"Fine. I'll arrange for Miss Rutledge to come in first thing in the morning. But I should warn you . . . Oliver McKenna knows about everything that's happening in this part of New Mexico. And he's very dangerous. I speak from experience. It's likely that he knows you're here."

"I'm certain he knows I'm here," Josh replied. "I had the dubious privilege of meeting one of his employees today . . . Mr. Frank Crenshaw."

Danna's brow wrinkled with concern. "Crenshaw? He ramrods McKenna's hired guns. You didn't have any trouble?"

"A bit." Josh gave Danna a sketchy narrative of what had taken place at the saloon.

When he finished, she said, "They know that you're in my office then. They'll know a lot more. Like I said, be careful. Very careful."

6

THE RIVERS BROTHERS strolled down the wagon-rutted street toward Danna Sinclair's law office. They were an unlikely pair. Josh was immaculately dressed in a dark gray suit which appeared out of place in the bright, early morning sun that had started baking the sleepy cow town. Cal was something of a dandy in contrasting style, wearing a fresh, light buckskin shirt which seemed molded to his muscular torso.

They had walked silently after leaving their hotel, each lost in his thoughts. The quietness was natural between them, Josh thought, for the Rivers children had been raised not to crowd each other with too much talk. "You can say a hell of a lot by not talking," Levi always used to say, "and learn a hell of a lot more by listening."

As they angled toward the boardwalk in front of Danna's office, the hair on the back of Josh's neck suddenly bristled, and instinctively, his hand edged under his coat toward the butt of his Peacemaker revolver.

"You're getting rusty, Josh," Cal said. "I smelled trouble a couple of minutes ago."

"This is a hell of a time to play games," Josh said as they quickened their pace.

Glass shattered behind them, and Josh's pistol sprung into his hand at the same instant a rifle cracked. He whirled, his gun probing the air looking for a target. He caught sight of the broken window in the second story of the feed warehouse across the street, but the gunman was out of view.

“Son of a bitch," Josh muttered angrily. He glanced over his shoulder and saw his brother sprawled face-down in the dusty street. "Cal?"

Cal stirred and raised himself up on his hands and began dragging himself inch by inch toward the boardwalk. Josh backed slowly toward him, his eyes darting warily from door to door and window to window of the buildings that lined the opposite side of the street. "You're hit?" he asked the obvious as he crouched beside Cal, his gun still poised to fire. He saw the color fading from his brother's face and the pain burning in his eyes.

Cal leaned up against the edge of the boardwalk and nodding toward his hip, grimaced in pain. "You're goddamned right, I'm hit. But that isn't the worst of it. I took a bullet in the butt. The bushwhacking bastard. He couldn't even hit me someplace dignified."

Josh saw that he was bleeding badly. Dark crimson soaked the right leg of Cal's trousers. "We've got to get you inside," Josh said.

Just then, the door of Danna Sinclair's office opened as if in response. Danna and a slender older woman with ginger colored hair, who Josh assumed was Dawn Rutledge, stepped cautiously through the door. He was taken aback momentarily at the sight of the shiny new Winchester in Danna's hands.

"The window," Danna gasped and, raising her rifle, fired.

Josh sprang to his feet and hammered off two quick shots at the skulking figure in the warehouse window. The man pitched forward, the remaining shards of glass crashing around him, and he hung there, suspended from the window ledge for a moment, before he slipped from the sill and plummeted to the street.

Josh heard the thudding of boots moving quickly across the warehouse floor. "He had a friend," he said, holstering his pistol, "but I think he's lost interest."

With the help of the two women, Josh carried Cal inside and lowered him onto the bed in Danna's living quarters. No sooner had Cal's heavy frame sunk into the mattress than Danna was slashing away at his blood-soaked trousers with a pearl-handled knife, the likes of which Josh had never seen before. It was a wicked-looking weapon, he thought, a dagger of some type which could be folded back into the handle when not in use. And the deftness of her hands indicated that Danna Sinclair was quite comfortable with the weapon. She had seemed at home looking into the sights of the Winchester, too. An intriguing woman.

Josh and Dawn Rutledge shifted Cal on the bed while Danna finished removing the shredded trousers, leaving the lower half of his body naked and exposed.

"I was damned worried about the way you were swinging that knife around," Cal said, his voice a near whisper. "For a while, I was afraid you were going to take more than my pants."

"I didn't see anything worth taking," Danna said with a straight face.

Cal was apparently not wounded too badly, Josh thought, because he hadn't lost his sense of humor. But he seemed to have met his match in Danna Sinclair.

Dawn Rutledge brought some rags and a porcelain basin full

of water to the bedside, and Danna began to wash the blood away from Cal's white buttocks. The bleeding was only a trickle now, Josh noted, but the bullet had made a nasty wound.

"The bullet will have to come out," Danna said matter-of-factly. "Doc Middleton's office is across from The Longhorn, Josh."

She did not tell him to fetch the doctor, or ask him, but he got her message.

7

WHEN HE ENTERED Dr. Homer Middleton's office, Josh walked into a large room that apparently served the physician as a combined reception and examination room and surgery. The room was scantily furnished and the medical equipment and supplies could have been crammed into a single closet.

At first he thought the doctor was out, perhaps called away on another emergency. Then his body tensed at the sound of deep, almost labored breathing from behind a curtained area in the far corner.

"Dr. Middleton?" he called tentatively. There was no reply, but someone was behind the curtain; the sound was unmistakable in the deathly quiet of the room.

Josh drew his pistol and stepped cautiously, softly, across the room. When he reached the curtain, he stood there for a moment, waiting, listening. The rhythmic pace of the breathing had not changed and he could detect no other movement. Josh grabbed the curtain and flung it back. He relaxed and slid his pistol back into its holster when he saw the rotund, bald man with the white Van Dyke beard stretched out on the wooden table. The man was lost in deep slumber, his ample belly rising and falling like the wheezing of a blacksmith's bellows.

Josh cleared his throat, but got no reaction. "I'm looking for Dr. Middleton," he said, his voice even. He received a few jumbled snorts and grunts, but otherwise, no response. He reached over and shook the man's shoulders harshly, and this time, in a stern, loud voice said, "I'm looking for Dr. Middleton."

The elderly man's eyes popped open. In a single motion he jolted upright and swung his feet over the table's edge, moving faster than Josh would have imagined him capable. As the old man stepped onto the dust-coated floor, anger blazed in his eyes and he shouted, "Damn crazy fool! Don't you have better sense than to sneak up on a man like that? You nearly frightened the bloody piss out of me . . . that's what you did."

"I'm trying to find Dr. Middleton," Josh said. "You're the closest thing to life that I've found in this room."

"None too close, young man," he replied, "but you have found him. I am Dr. Middleton." He straightened and threw back his shoulders, making a ceremony of brushing and smoothing his rumpled coat and trousers. Then he seemed to be studying Josh with interest and he could feel himself being sized up under the other man's scrutinizing eyes.

"How can I be of service?" the doctor asked. "You look as healthy as Mable Crockett's prize stallion. In fact, you look so goddamned healthy, you make me sick."

"It's my brother. He's been shot." A cloud of genuine concern swept over the doctor's face. The old fart was softer than he let on.

Dr. Middleton hurried across the room to a warped cupboard. "How bad?"

"Bad enough," Josh said, "but he's not dying. He took a bullet in the cheek of his butt. He's on the bed in Miss Sinclair's quarters."

The doctor shook his head in disbelief, chuckling to himself now as he rummaged through the cupboard, seemingly stuffing all of its meager contents into a traditional black, leather bag. "Did she shoot him?"

"Who?"

"Danna. Danna Sinclair. Is she the one who shot your brother?"

"No, no of course not. Why would you think that?"

"Danna . . . Miss Sinclair . . . is not a woman to be trifled with," the doctor said as they started up the street toward the Sinclair law office. "She takes very little shit from any man, or woman, for that matter. She's as sharp as a porcupine's quill, and she's not fooled by anybody."

"I can believe that," Josh said. "From what I've seen, she's one tough lady who can take care of herself anyplace."

"That's true. But don't get me wrong. She's got a gentle side, if you give her gentleness. With Danna, you get what you give. Give her honesty and you get it back. Stab her in the back; watch your own." Dr. Middleton chuckled again. "I meant that literally, Some dumb bastard tried to give her what she didn't want a week or so back. You heard about it, I suppose."

"No, I just rode in yesterday."

"Well, it's too much of a story to tell now, but it seems this fellow had the idea he was going to kill Danna. But he tried to have his way with her first. Danna tore into him like a goddamned Comanche and sliced him to pieces with that toad-stabber of hers. Among other things, she circumcised the bastard . . . about an inch too far back."

"Well, I'll be damned," Josh said, half in shock, half in admiration.

The doctor stopped at Danna's door and turned to Josh. "Just who are you, young man?" he asked bluntly.

Josh extended his hand "Josh Rivers. I'm a lawyer from Santa Fe."

The doctor answered with a firm grip and cocked his head to one side, crinkling his brow professorially. "Rivers," he said, rolling the name off his tongue. "Any relation to Levi Rivers of the Slash R?"

"His third son."

The doctor nodded his head as if entering into an unspoken agreement. "We'll get along," he said, "we'll get along just fine."

8

CAL RIVERS SLUMBERED under the effects of laudanum with Dawn Rutledge at his bedside while Josh and Dr. Middleton joined Danna in her outer office. "He should be fine in a few days," Dr. Middleton announced, wiping at his sweat-beaded brow with a crumpled white handkerchief. "He's a remarkable specimen of a man." He looked at Danna with a twinkle in his blue eyes. "Don't you agree, Danna?"

Danna could feel the heat of her face flushing. She agreed. She had not been totally clinical in her appraisal of Cal Rivers's lean, sinewy body. Physically, he was a man who took your breath away, powerfully built, flawlessly handsome, but she was not about to concede her intrigue to Doc Middleton. "I hadn't noticed," she said curtly, cursing him with her eyes before she turned to Josh. "How does this affect our business?" she asked.

Dr. Middleton closed his black bag and moved toward the door. "I'll stop back this afternoon," he said.

"No, wait, Doc," Danna said. "I'd like you to stay for a few moments." She turned to Josh and explained, "He's a friend. You can trust Doc with your life. And he knows why you're here."

Josh nodded assent. "Now, as far as our business is concerned, we'll just have to make some changes in our plans. I guess I'll be riding out of here alone tomorrow morning. Cal's not going to be sitting in the saddle for a spell, and from what I've learned, maybe it's just as well."

"What do you mean?"

"Dr. Middleton tells me that there's already been one attempt made on your life. I think it's just as well that Cal stays close till I get back."

Her eyes sparked. "I don't need any man looking after me. I was raised on a South Texas ranch. My father saw to it that I could handle weapons as well as any man . . . better than most." She was angry. She had thought Josh Rivers was a different cut of man, one who did not treat her womanliness condescendingly.

"Don't be so damned touchy," Josh said. "I'd sure as hell rather have Cal riding next to me. But anybody can get shot, man or woman. Look at Cal. He's as tough and wily as anybody in the Southwest, but that didn't stop him from taking a bullet. I'm just saying that two guns are better than one."

Meeting the even gaze of his dark eyes, she saw no mockery there, and her temper cooled. "Your brother can stay here until he's well enough to move to the hotel," she said. "Within two weeks I'll have to go to Santa Fe to appear before Judge Robinson. He can ride along if he's well enough to travel."

"He should be," Dr. Middleton interjected. "He'll have a tender butt for quite some time, but in a few weeks, he should be able to ride . . . with some padding in the right places."

"Since you're going to Santa Fe anyway," Josh said, "I'd like to offer a suggestion and make a request, if I may."

"What is it?" Danna asked.

"Stay there until I return. You can use my office library. It will be convenient . . . and safer. Besides, Oliver McKenna might own Madison, but he doesn't own Santa Fe. Cal and I have friends there. Can you be away from your office that long?"

She smiled wryly. "I don't know. The mice might get hungry in my absence. I have so few clients that I doubt my absence will even be noticed."

"I can keep an eye on things here," Dr. Middleton said. "If I hear of anything that might be of interest to you, I'll get word to you in Santa Fe. I'll need to know where to contact you."

"At my office," Josh said. Then turning to Danna, "That brings me to my request. Would you consider looking after my practice while I'm gone? I have a crotchety old law clerk running the office right now. He may bristle a bit at first, but I've been neglecting my clients too long, and if somebody doesn't tend to business, some of them are going to jump the traces. I'm a greedy man; I want to keep my clients."

There was no work waiting for her in Madison, and that is what she wanted: work. Legal work. She quickly pondered her options.

"I'll make it financially worth your while." Josh said.

"Yes," Danna replied, without further hesitation, "I'll look after your office until your return. Consider it done." She extended her hand, and when Josh received it, she had a strange feeling that the handshake was more than acknowledgement of a casual agreement. She released his hand with an unexplainable sense that more than a transitory bonding had taken place between them. The feeling did not unnerve her in the least. For some reason, Josh Rivers was a man she discovered that she trusted.

9

JOSH REINED IN his buckskin gelding, tugged his low-crowned hat down over his forehead, and squinted into the blinding sun that hovered just above the western horizon. He sat easily in the saddle, but his eyes were intense and his senses alert as he scanned the gray prairie that spread out before him. He waited. Perhaps he had been hearing things. A week alone on the Llano Estacado, known by some as the Staked Plains, could do that to a man.

He wished Cal were with him. "If you're looking for Kwahadi this time of year," Cal had said, "head for the Staked Plains. If you don't find them, sooner or later, they'll find you." Josh knew his brother was right, and he had picked up plenty of Kwahadi signs as he crisscrossed the barren, wrinkled ground of this seemingly forgotten part of northwest Texas. Cal would have located a village by now, but instead of tracking Comanche, he was probably lulling in luxury at the Exchange Hotel in Santa Fe, properly attended, of course, by ladies of his choice. "I'll be fine, big brother," Cal had said with a wicked smile on his face, "as long as I keep my butt in the air."

Suddenly, Josh shivered, and a chill danced down his spine.

He had heard screams. They were faint, yet shrill, piercing, like the eerie calling of mountain cats in the night. But Josh Rivers had heard such cries before and knew they were uttered from human throats. They were animal sounds, mindless and unintelligible, borne of the deepest agony and despair, pleading for the mercy that could only be delivered by death.

Then he caught sight of the smoke: black, billowy clouds that rose from the earth, and then feathered out and disappeared into the sweep of the hot Texas wind. He swiped his dust-caked arms across his forehead, trying to ward off the stinging sweat that dripped into his eyes.

Comanche. From the signs he had been reading, they should not have been this close. On the other hand, he thought wryly, Comanche were never where they were supposed to be.

Josh edged the buckskin toward the jagged spine of the ridge that snaked its way north and west in the direction of the smoke. Moving in behind the cover afforded by the mesquite-shrouded ridge, he dismounted and cautiously led the horse along the rocky base of the slope. As he advanced, the incessant screaming grew louder, more hideous.

The Comanche were imaginative torturers. Josh could only speculate as to what was happening to the poor devils out there. It would not be a pretty sight.

He stopped, and after hitching his horse to a clump of brush, clambered up the side of a dune-like formation where the peak of the ridge began to taper off into the parched ocean of prairie. He peered through a break in the rock, his face impassive as he appraised the scene that unfolded perhaps a hundred yards in front of him: a stagecoach, a fancy Concorde.

The coach, or what was left of it, lay on its side. It was aflame, but Josh could make out the bright gold and crimson of the varnished panels through the smoke. He had ridden in several similar luxurious models used by the Overland Express on its more prosperous runs. But there weren't any stage routes in this part of Texas.

He could make out the ruts of a trail that led to and from the site of the massacre. That would have to be the Cimarron cutoff, the treacherous shortcut branch of the Santa Fe Trail that prudent travelers avoided unless they were extremely well armed and well supplied. But only fools would take a lone stagecoach across the hazard-ridden cutoff.

Josh's eyes focused on the activity around the smoldering coach. They were Comanche, all right. Four of them. Probably a scouting party that just happened upon the stage.

Off to one side, sprawled over a dead horse that would have been one of the six-horse team, was the still form of a man, a white man from his dress, Josh guessed. Two barebacked Indians, one clad in cavalry breeches, no doubt a trophy from some past raid, were absorbed in harnessing and gathering up the remaining horses.

The real prize here would be the horses, for no Plains Indians exceeded the Comanche in their love for the horse. Josh had heard the Comanche compared to the mythical Centaur, half-horse, half-man, so skilled and dexterous was he with the animal. Indeed, a Comanche on a horse seemed grafted to the creature, moving and reacting to the horse's rhythm and gait like an appendage upon its back.

He glanced back at his own powerfully built, thickly muscled horse. Comanche warriors would kill enthusiastically for an animal like the buckskin.

Turning his eyes to the stage, Josh caught sight of two Comanche kneeling over several hapless victims like small boys preoccupied with a game. There were two white men, spread-eagled on the ground, and Josh shuddered to think what Comanche devilment was eliciting the unrelenting, hysterical screaming from their throats. The men were well on their way to dying, but they would be at it for a long time.

Still, there was nothing he could do for them. It wasn't his fight. It would make no sense for him to risk his own neck on a mission that would not change the final outcome.

Then he caught a glimpse of a woman on the far side of the stage. She had been partially concealed by the haze of smoke. She appeared to be dazed or stunned as she sat on the earth, her head bowed, her hands lashed behind her back. But she was a woman. There was no doubt about that.

Her flowing black hair gleamed like shiny coal in the torrid sun, and he could make out the remnants of her scarlet-red dress that had been ripped away from her shoulders, leaving her milk-white skin exposed to the merciless wind and sun.

The Comanche were ignoring her for the moment, and chances were they planned to take her with them if she did not prove to be too much of a nuisance. They tended to take women and children captive if they were strong and healthy and showed some evidence they might be worthy of eventual adoption by the band.

The great Kwahadi war chief, Quanah Parker himself, was the son of a white captive who had been abducted as a child by the Comanche.

The attackers were most likely Kwahadi, for at the Grand Peace Council at Medicine Creek, Kansas in 1867, most of the

Comanche bands and the neighboring Kiowa had agreed to cede their homeland and go to a reservation in the Indian territory. Quanah had not. He and his disciples had blazed a trail of blood across West Texas and eastern New Mexico in the years since.

The woman put a different light on things. Josh pushed himself back and slid down the slope to his horse and eased into the saddle. There weren't any options to consider: he had to charge the Comanche head on.

Most Comanche were poorly armed and couldn't shoot worth a damn. It was a risk. They might kill the woman, but he was gambling they'd be more worried about getting away with the horses.

Josh slipped his Peacemaker out of its holster and kicked the gelding gently in the flanks. The horse burst forward and Josh swung around the rim and charged at a dead run across the prairie towards the burning stagecoach. He was midway between the ridge and coach before he was sighted by one of the warriors who rose up from the victim he had been crouched over and began yelling frantically to his comrades.

Josh fired off two wild shots, holstered the pistol, and in a single fluid motion, without breaking the gait of his horse, pulled his Winchester from its saddle holster. The Comanche broke for their horses, with the exception of one who leaped through the flaming remnants of the coach and dashed for the woman, his war axe posed to strike. Josh pulled the buckskin up short, and the horse wheeled and stopped.

"Hold tight, Bucky," Josh murmured as he lifted the Winchester to his shoulder and squeezed the trigger. The rifle cracked, and the Comanche bolted upright as though a sledge had been driven into his back. Then he pitched forward and collapsed just inches from the seemingly oblivious woman.

Josh's expertise with the rifle was a gift from Levi Rivers. The horse was an extra limb to the Comanche; the rifle was an additional arm to the members of the Rivers clan.

The remaining Comanche swooped onto their horses, gathered up the stage mounts, and raced away under a curtain of swirling, red dust. Josh rode up to the remains of the charred, smoldering stage, his eyes smarting from the acrid smoke that chased him wherever he moved. His ears rang from the echoing screams of the two men stretched out on the barren earth in front of him.

Dismounting, he saw instantly that the dead man was luckiest of the three. A glance at the woman on the far side of the rubble told him she was unharmed . . . physically, at least.

He moved to the side of the nearer man. He was a sallow-skinned man, with black hair, a precisely trimmed mustache, and dark eyes that stared blankly skyward from a face that was a mask of horror. "You'll be all right," Josh said, knowing his reassurance was a lie. "I'm a friend."

The man kept screaming as if unaware of Josh's presence. Josh fought off the urge to retch as his eyes scanned the mutilated body. The Comanche's knives had cut away the man's elegant clothes and peeled them back, much as one might skin a rabbit. Then they had butchered. Dark red blood gurgled like lava from a volcano where the man's genitals had been before brutal amputation, and a knot of bluish gut protruded from the filleted groin. As he sliced away the rawhide strips that anchored the pathetic man to the wooden stakes that pinned him to the ground, Josh saw that the crimson that painted the man's neck was erupting from his mouth, and suddenly realized that the poor soul was about to drown in his own blood. What could a man without a tongue do but scream?

When Josh freed him, the man began to choke and sob, his screams subsiding to moans and groans of agony as he writhed in pain on the ground. Josh moved quickly to the other victim, a bald, stocky man whose naked abdomen had suffered a similar fate and whose vacant eye sockets were pools of overflowing scarlet. "They're gone," Josh said, again his voice trying to sooth. "I'll have you free in a minute."

The rotund man stopped his shrieking, was silent a moment as he bit on his lower lip till blood came, and then croaked, "I can't take it mister. Oh, God, finish me off." He began to cry like a frightened child. "Please," he blubbered. "Oh, goddamn, I can't stand it."

Josh did not bother to untie the bonds. He stood and drew the Peacemaker, pointing the pistol at the man's head. He pulled back the hammer and squeezed the trigger. After the explosion, a strange smile formed on the dead man's lips, and his body relaxed, and his agony was ended.

Josh turned back to the other man and just as quickly ended his suffering. If he would have done as much for a horse, why not a man?

Josh cast a wary look in the direction the Comanche had fled. They would return as soon as they had secured the stolen mounts, for it was not fear for their lives that had sent them running. Comanche were practical people, fiercely brave, but not foolhardy. They would first seek to preserve the plunder they had gained and then return to deal with the white-eyes on their own terms.

He could likely handle three of them, but if they were near the main band, his troubles were just starting.

Josh hurried over to the woman and was surprised to find her staring at him. As he moved to her, he saw more curiosity than fear in the pair of alert, jade-green eyes. "Are you alright, ma'am?" Josh asked as he knelt and sliced the rawhide bonds with his Bowie knife.

"I will be," she replied evenly, "as soon as we get the hell out of here."

She stumbled to her feet with Josh's assistance and then stepped away and began tugging the bodice of her dress into some semblance of order. She seemed relatively unruffled by her experience and did not appear embarrassed as he watched her rearrange the fabric of her torn dress in a vain effort to cover her large, well-formed breasts.

She looked up at him, smiling wanly. "Do you suppose you could help?" she asked.

Josh hesitated only momentarily. "Yes, of course," and he moved to her side, and with the rawhide strips that had bound her wrists, fashioned a crude shoulder strap and tied it to the torn fabric of the bodice of the dress to hold it in place.

"You're very handy," she said when he had finished. She extended her hand. "I'm Jessica Chandler."

He accepted it. "Josh Rivers."

Her eyes traveled the length of his body like a horse trader appraising a stallion. "You're very handsome," she said. "Filthy, but handsome."

Josh could not restrain the faint traces of a smile. The woman had come within inches of death and had been through an experience, the shock of which would have permanently addled the brain of some women, yet she was interested in his appearance.

"Thank you, ma'am," he replied. "You're a beautiful woman . . . filthy, but beautiful."

She flashed a mischievous smile. "At least you don't look like you're going to scalp me."

"No, but if we don't move out of here *pronto*, we'll meet up with some of the scalping kind sooner than we want. We've got one horse between us. We'll have to ride double and that will slow us down. I want to head for Big Sandy Creek. We'll find water and hiding places there. If we can make it that far, we have a good chance."

His eyes roamed over the silent corpses that were strewn about. "We won't have time to bury these men. I'm sorry we can't do more."

Her face turned glum, but this tall woman, who was slender to the point of seeming fragile, had a backbone of cold, hard steel. "I understand," she said. "They're dead; we're alive. I'd just as soon keep it that way."

10

THE SUN HAD slipped behind the horizon when they made camp in one of the dense groves of green ash that covered the bottomlands of the Big Sandy. As they rested in the shifting shadows of the trees, Josh tossed Jessica Chandler a ration of hardtack and beef jerky.

"It isn't a gourmet meal," he said, "but it will help keep your strength up."

She nodded assent and attacked his offering with a ferocity that belied her delicate femininity.

As they ate, Josh gazed up through motionless branches of ash that split the starlit sky. The full moon would be a glowing lantern when it reached its peak this July night. They would have been easily spotted on the open prairie, and he had breathed easier since reaching refuge in the trees. Now they had some cover if they had to make a stand.

He had not picked up any signs of pursuit yet. Perhaps the Indians had been discouraged by the darkness. Comanche were unpredictable about night-fighting. Some shared the sentiments of their cousins, the Apaches, who believed that the spirits of warriors killed in the darkness of night were doomed to wander lost and aimless for eternity. As far as Josh knew, the belief was not a dogmatic tenet of the Comanche religion, and he doubted Quanah Parker cared what time of day he took a white man's scalp.

"Mr. Rivers," Jessica Chandler said, pulling Josh away from his musing.

"Yes, ma'am?"

"Could you spare a drink of water?"

He saw that she had wolfed down her food. "Sure, we have plenty of water, and if we stay with the creek, that'll be the least of our troubles."

He got up and walked over to the buckskin to retrieve his canteen from the saddle. She had a pleasant voice, soft, yet very clear. She had spoken hardly a word since they rode away from the carnage left by the Comanche. Without complaint, she had endured the whipping winds and baking heat that sucked out the strength from the strongest man. Her butt and crotch had to be bruised raw from the jostling she had taken from straddling the big buckskin over some of the roughest country in western Texas, but she had clung to him tenaciously as she rode behind him with her dress hiked up to the shapeliest thighs he had ever seen. The closest she had come to protest was a whispered "damn" when Bucky lost his footing on the rocky trail that led from the higher plateau lands to the lower banks of the Big Sandy. He did not know what to make of her yet, but she had grit; he had to give her credit for that.

After handing Jessica the canteen, he sat down a few feet from her so they could speak softly. "You didn't have to wait on me," she said. "I could have gotten it myself."

"I know."

"I thought you were a ruffian when we first met. A handsome one, but a ruffian nonetheless. I was wrong. You're a gentleman. Obviously, a man of education and breeding. What in heaven's name are you doing in this god-forsaken country, Mr. Rivers?"

"Let's just say I'm looking for someone. And call me Josh."

"If you call me Jessica." She hesitated. "I imagine you would like to know how I came to be in this predicament."

"It's none of my business," he said. And he meant it. He was curious; he could not deny that. But he did not push his way into a person's private rooms, and he did not expect others to shove their way into his.

"But I think it is your business since you've taken me on as your burden. In any event I would like to tell you." Josh nodded assent. "I'm with a theatrical company," she said, "or I was. The old man, the one with the beard, he was our driver and jack-of-all-trades. The bald-headed man's name was George Beeson. He owned the company and was quite a good actor on occasion. The third man was my husband, Francis Colette." She looked pensive but showed no remorse. "I guess I'm a widow now. It's a strange feeling. It's rather difficult to think of myself as a widow."

"I'm sorry," Josh said, "I didn't know."

"I suppose you think I'm behaving very coldly about the whole thing."

Josh did not reply, letting her decide if she wanted to explain. She did.

"My husband was a very fine actor when he was sober . . . which was not often. He was once quite prominent on the New York stage. I met him twenty years ago in St. Louis. I was fifteen; he was twenty years older than me. I wanted to be an actress and I wanted to leave St. Louis, so I pursued him. The leading lady with the troop had taken ill and returned to the East. As usual, Beeson's company was on the financial brink. They needed someone to play the lead role in Mazeppa. Are you familiar with it?"

"Not as a play. It's a poem, isn't it? By Lord Byron?"

"I was right. You are a literate man. I think I'm going to find you interesting, Josh. But back to the play . . . it's based upon Byron's poem about a young Polish nobleman who, by implication at least, has an illicit liaison with an influential duke's wife. The duke treats Mazeppa like the proverbial fox in the chicken house and has him bound naked to a magnificent white stallion."

"Yes, I remember," Josh said. "And the stallion carries the young lover to Russia where he is eventually rescued by the Cossacks and rises to some prominence in his adopted country."

"Yes. I played Mazeppa."

"I don't quite see you as a young man."

"Oh, it wasn't all that difficult. I had some talent as an acrobat. That's what won me the part . . . and the husband. I wasn't actually tied naked to the horse; I wore flesh-colored tights. My breasts posed a bit of a problem and had to be bound, of course."

Josh found himself fascinated by Jessica's uninhibited speech and was content to let her carry the conversation.

"But about my husband. He was very dashing when I first met him. He had a fine education, and he taught me a great deal. My formal education left much to be desired, and I guess I was something of a challenge to him in that respect. Francis became obsessed with making a sophisticated woman out of me. He insisted that I have a proper command of language, and that I be well read in the classics. I was to do more than mouth the words of the characters in the plays. He wanted me to understand the meaning of those words, why the playwright put them there, what he was saying when he wrote them."

"I suspect he was a good teacher," Josh said.

"An excellent teacher but a terrible husband. And I was a worse wife. After a few weeks of marriage I found that his preferences were, shall I say, not female. And the bottle was his master. I also learned that I was a shrew. Shakespeare could not have written a more despicable one. But our marriage was a convenience, and we finally negotiated a civilized arrangement that was nearer to teacher-pupil than husband-wife. Francis and I would have parted ways, though, soon. On my part, our relationship was not a till-death-do-us-part one. The company was scheduled to play in Santa Fe. We were to do Hamlet; I was to be Ophelia. It's one of my favorite roles. She was a romantic. Deep down I think all actresses are. I hadn't told anyone, but after our week in Santa Fe, I planned to go east . . . either to Washington or New York." She sighed but did not seem all that perturbed. "This changes my plans, of course. My money, everything I owned . . . which wasn't much . . . burned with the stagecoach. But I got away with my life. Francis and the others didn't do that. It was a terrible end . . . especially for men who have spent their entire lifetimes in such a gentle pursuit. And the suffering they went through—"

"I wasn't sure how much you were aware of," Josh said. "You seemed to be in a daze when I rode in."

She was indignant. "Then I fooled you as well as I did the Indians. I wasn't in a daze; I was very much alert. I'm an actress. I resisted for a time, but then it occurred to me that the savages had no cause to be patient with a troublesome woman, so I slumped to the ground and entered into an appropriate trance-like state. Then they lost interest in me."

"They probably would have taken you captive if they decided you weren't a troublemaker. You would have become some warrior's squaw."

"Perhaps. But I would have been alive," she said simply. "There was no way I could help the others, so I helped myself. That doesn't sound very noble, does it?"

"I suppose not, but it sounds damned smart."

Josh retrieved his bedroll and spread it out near the fire. "It's warm now, but it'll start to get chilly and damp in another hour. You'll be glad to be near the hot coals tonight. Now, I'm going to walk down to the creek and wash up. I feel as filthy as you said I look."

She smiled impishly. "I didn't mean to drive you to a bath."

He smiled back. "It won't hurt much," he said as he picked up his saddle bags and headed toward the creek.

He worked his way along the trail to the soft, lush grass that edged the creek bank until he found a likely spot to bathe. The creek, with its sandy bottom, was crystal clear and ran slow and shallow in July. But the hole here should be waist high, deep enough to let him soak and soothe his weary bones.

He stripped naked and slipped into the water, lying back into its refreshing coolness until he was swallowed by its depths. Then he scrubbed the grime from his body, using the flesh of a yucca plant for crude soap. The soft caress of the gently swirling waters awakened and invigorated him, making him forget that he had slept no more than a dozen hours in the last five days.

"Is there room in the tub for two?" The teasing voice came from the creek bank.

Josh looked up and caught his breath at the sight of Jessica

Chandler standing there, her hands on her hips, unabashed, brazen, in her nakedness. Not even the creek's cold water could smother the heat that surged in his loins at the sight of her.

Her limbs were long, a bit gangly, but not in a way that detracted from her grace. Her breasts, uplifted, with prominent nipples, were full and sculptured. Her hips, although small, were well-rounded, gently tapering into her thighs.

She stood there, like the actress she was, basking in the soft, orange glow of the moonlight that seemed to shine solely upon her stage. "Do you have soap?" she asked.

"Yucca," he replied. "It makes good soap. The Indians use it."

"Good," she said, splashing into the water. "You can scrub my back."

And he did scrub her back. And her breasts. And her smooth, flat belly. Jessica responded with appreciative purrs and sighs. Josh found himself at once seduced and confounded by this breathtaking, incredibly beautiful widow of only a few hours. He would have been respectful of her grief, if she had shown the need. He lived by a simple code: he took from a woman only when she freely gave and took from him in return. Sex, in his lawyer's mind, was like a good contract, with mutuality as its core. And he had no doubt that Jessica Chandler was ready to contract.

When they emerged from the creek, they picked up their clothes and walked hurriedly, silently, back to their camp. The tightness of her grip of his hand told Josh that she shared in his urgency.

They reached the clearing where the dying campfire flickered like a candle in an open window. He saw that the blankets of the bedroll had been tossed back. He looked at her eyes that sparkled wickedly.

"At least you won't have to sacrifice your bedroll tonight," she said, pulling him down onto the blankets.

"I'm glad of that," he replied as he was received into her open arms. He kissed her long and deeply, quickening to the probing of her tongue, to the pressing of her pliant flesh against his own.

Abruptly she pulled her head back. "Please," she whispered imploringly.

He entered her and her body molded to his own. Her nails dug violently into his back and raked furrows over his ribs and down his buttocks and back again. She arched her back and thrust against him frantically, and he responded to her frenzy, driving himself deep within her, meeting her thrusts with equal fervor.

Their coupling was urgent and mechanical, and was concluded swiftly. She shuddered and tremors erupted over the length of her body in the same moment he released himself in a series of long, intense spasms. Exhausted, sated, they collapsed in each other's arms and fell instantly to sleep.

11

When Josh awakened, the morning sun beamed through the tree tops. The ashes in the fire were cold, but the sun's brilliant rays were already toasting the earth. He glanced at Jessica who was snuggled close to him, her head cradled against his chest. He placed his hand gently on her forehead and brushed a wisp of soft hair from her face. Her eyes opened lazily at his touch. He wanted her again, and her eyes said she wanted him. He moved his hand tentatively to her breast and then suddenly froze.

The little glen was deathly quiet, void of the usual morning sounds of birds chirping in the trees, squirrels scrambling in the branches. Comanche quiet.

"What is it?" Jessica whispered.

Josh did not reply as he reached for the holstered pistol that lay next to the bedroll. They had slept for better than ten hours, a dangerous, stupid thing to do in Comanche land, and now they would pay for it. He pulled his hand back weaponless, however, when he saw the Comanche, seven or eight of them, emerge from the trees.

"Oh, my God," Jessica gasped, terror in her eyes.

"Stay calm," Josh said softly. "This is going to take your best performance."

He rose from the blankets, feeling ridiculous as he stood there in total nakedness to greet the Indians, who stared at him with sinister and solemn faces. Josh waited, meeting their gazes unflinchingly, making no gesture, knowing the safest course was to let the Comanche make the first move.

Finally, a tall man with regal bearing, clad in a simple breechclout and buckskin war shirt and calf-high moccasins, stepped toward Josh, a rifle cradled menacingly in his arms. He was taller and heavier-boned than most Comanche Josh had encountered. He was a handsome man by any standards. His high cheekbones, angular face, and coffee-brown skin left no doubt that Comanche blood ran in his veins. Only the penetrating steel-blue eyes betrayed the white side of Quanah Parker's heritage.

12

DANNA HEARD THE splash of water, the dull thud of weight, against the bathtub in her bedroom. At the sound of Cal's pained "goddamn," she pushed her chair back from the desk and went into the bedroom where Cal had been savoring his first real bath in two weeks.

"What's the matter?" she called, her voice stern. She had a feeling that Calvin Rivers was far from the invalid he claimed to be.

He was well enough to have tried a dozen devious tricks to lure her into bed three days after Doc Middleton had removed the bullet. She had pulled back the covers on the bed to give Cal the sponge bath which she administered faithfully twice a day. She had helped him over on his side, then felt herself flush with embarrassment, an emotion not common to her nature, when she saw his enormous male organ swollen in granite hardness. Cal had just smiled impishly and shrugged. She had read the invitation in his eyes that gauged her for a reaction, before she regained her composure and tossed the sheet back over his naked hip. She left the water basin at his bedside and dropped the wet washrag on his bare chest. "I think you're well enough to take care of your own bath from now on," she had said simply and walked away.

She had relented some in her resolve, however, when he had moaned in agony as he tried to lift himself out of bed and when he tried to reach inaccessible parts of his long, lean body. She had become accustomed to his lack of modesty. While she was not uncomfortable with his casual nudity, neither was she immune to it. If Cal Rivers were only a little more subtle in his approach, somewhat less obvious, she would find the total maleness of him nearly impossible to resist.

She stood over him now, and he looked up at her, half swallowed by the water in the tub, a grimace on his face. "I slipped. Came down on my butt," he said. "It's killing me."

"Do you need help getting out?" she asked, but she caught the wicked glint in his eyes before he spoke.

"Well, I'm not quite as far along as I thought I was. Maybe you could stay and help me over to the bed."

She snatched up the towel and leaned over to help him out of the tub. He clasped a hand upon her shoulder as he tried to brace himself, and then suddenly his other arm swung around her neck and he pulled her head to his as she struggled to keep from tumbling into the tub. His mouth closed over hers and, for an instant, she held the kiss from the lips that were, at once, gentle and firm, coaxing and demanding. But then she felt his hand upon her breast, grasping hungrily, and a part of her ached to surrender to the racing of her own blood.

But no. Not like this. He was taking her, and she would not be taken. Not by any man.

She pulled back, but he held onto one arm. "Now come on, sweetheart," he said. "I've seen the way you look at me. You're more woman than law wrangler."

Her green eyes flamed. The arrogant bastard! Her fist shot out, slamming him broadside on the nose. He released the grip on her other arm and cupped his hand over his nose as if to collect the dark red blood that came rushing out of one nostril. "Goddamn, you crazy woman."

She picked up a towel and tossed it over his head. "Lay your head back, stop the bleeding . . . then get out of the tub. You're a hell of a long way from needing my help, mister. Then get your pants on. I've seen enough of your bare butt these last two weeks to last me a lifetime."

She whirled and marched out of the room. "I'll be in my office; let me know when you're decent. It's time we had a talk."

When she returned a half hour later, Danna found the penitent Calvin Rivers, who sat at the table sipping a steaming cup of black coffee poured from a pot he had brewed himself. He poured Danna a cup as she sat down across the table from him. He looked like a young pup that had been swatted on the rump with a newspaper, she thought. He held a handkerchief across his nose, but it appeared that the bleeding had stopped. She must not have hurt him too badly. She was glad of that. She could not help but like Cal Rivers, now that her initial anger had passed. But she had better keep him at a distance.

Somehow, law was easier to handle than men, and she was not certain she could handle Cal Rivers . . . or if she wanted to.

"I guess I owe you an apology," he said contritely, as she accepted the proffered cup. His blue eyes met hers. They were affidavit eyes, she thought. The kind that could make you believe red was blue if he told you that.

He sucked in his breath. "So, I apologize."

"I accept your apology." Danna found it difficult to be as severe as she would like. "Now, so we don't have any future misunderstandings, I think I should explain a few things to you. First, I didn't take kindly to your remark that I was more woman than law wrangler. I find no inconsistency between the two. Second, no one touches me unless I want to be touched. Your brother and I are temporarily professional associates, and I guess you come as part of the package. But we're just in business together. That's all you have to remember." Her voice was firm and even, yet not scolding. "Can you remember that, Mr. Rivers?"

He looked at her with eyes that were sincere. "Yes, ma'am. I won't forget my place from now on."

He probably meant his words at the moment, Danna thought. She had no doubt that Cal Rivers was essentially an honorable man in most matters, but when it came to affairs of the flesh, she suspected his good intentions were easily brushed aside. But she could not vouch for her own resolve in the presence of this man. She held out her hand, and he accepted her firm grip. "We'll start over from this moment. We can begin with first names, if that's all right with you."

"I'd like that Danna, I'd like it fine."

"Good. Now, Cal," she said, "since your health has recovered so suddenly, I'm certain you won't mind if I reclaim the bed tonight. Alone. And I'll surrender the cot in my office to your use."

"Yes, ma'am." He smiled good-naturedly.

"Are you well enough to ride a horse?"

He rubbed his hip gingerly. "Most of me is. But I've got one tender butt."

"We're riding to Santa Fe the day after tomorrow; we'll leave just before dawn. I'm going to post a sign on my door tomorrow that I'll be absent from the office for an extended period beginning next week. Doc Middleton will discreetly try to encourage that belief. McKenna will catch on soon enough and send somebody after us, but maybe we can throw him off just long enough to get a head start."

She could tell he was looking at her skeptically. "You can't outrun anybody if we're going to take a buggy through that mountain road."

"There won't be any buggy. I believe you'll find I ride as well as you . . . probably better."

"I never did care for modest women," Cal replied with feigned sarcasm.

"We do have one problem," she said.

"What's that?"

"Dawn Rutledge. She's been staying in a boarding house here in Madison. She's enjoyed some safety in numbers, but sooner or later, Oliver McKenna's apt to take some notion that the best way to shut off the lawyers is to remove the client. She can't stay in Madison."

"Then she's coming with us?"

"I guess she'll have to. But Dawn says she rides only passably. She'll slow us down. I'm concerned that she won't be safe in Santa Fe, either. It won't be that difficult for a hired killer to reach her there."

Cal took a sip from his coffee cup and leaned back in his chair rubbing the back of his neck thoughtfully. After a few moments, he spoke. "She only needs to slow us up half the distance."

"What do you mean?"

"The Slash R's only a little bit out of the way. It would be a good stop for us anyhow; a place to run for and a place of rest and safety. There'll be fresh horses if we need them. Miss Rutledge can stay there until she's needed. She wouldn't be safer any place in New Mexico."

13

THEY HAD LEFT Dawn Rutledge with Levi Rivers at the Slash R. Miss Rutledge, an attractive, well-spoken woman in her mid-fifties had been the immediate target of Levi's charm. He had quickly ensconced her in the guest room of the big house, chaperoned, of course, by the cheerful, plump live-in Mexican housekeeper who welcomed the prospects of female companionship.

Cal and Danna took rooms for the night, but by morning Cal and Levi had obviously both had enough of the family reunion. At breakfast Levi had practically accused Cal of intentionally getting shot to avoid joining Josh in the search for Erin McKenna. "And taking a bullet in the ass to boot," he chided, shaking his head disgustedly.

Cal had gotten up from the table, gathered up his gear, and headed for the stable, calling back to Danna, "We ride out in fifteen minutes. I'll have your horse saddled up."

Levi shrugged. "That boy never could take a ribbing."

They had ridden out early that morning, hoping they could reach Santa Fe with no more than four nights on the trail. Cal figured a day and a half would likely put them out of range for Comanche trouble.

They were no more than six hours away from the Slash R ranch complex when Cal reined in his horse and signaled Danna to stop. He pointed toward the southeast. In the distance, seemingly tottering on the edge of the flat prairie, almost hidden behind the blooming cherry-red cholla and gray-green ironwood brush, the box-like adobe building looked like a tiny doll house, the empty corrals like miniature stick fences.

"Too damn quiet," Cal said, as they reined their horses to a slow trot and moved warily toward the lonely homestead that lay less than a half mile away.

"I know," Danna replied. "No horses in the corral, not a cow in sight."

"Probably deserted," Cal said. A sudden gust of wind struck from the west, scorching their faces like the hot blast of a furnace. Danna's eyes caught Cal's instantly. There was nothing to be said; the wind had answered their questions.

It had been a dozen years since she smelled a death wind, but the memory of it was branded in her mind. Its message was clear. She stiffened in the saddle and steeled herself for what lay ahead.

As they rode up to the edge of the ranch yard, the dollhouse faded and turned into a real home, crude and bleak as it was. Just as real was the stench that hovered like a swamp fog over the homestead, biting at their eyes till tears came, tearing at their throats till the bile rose. And the mutilated bodies stripped to slate-white bone at places where turkey vultures had eaten their fill before sweeping away for a siesta. Another day in the searing sun, exposed to the scavengers of the Texas prairie, and there would be nothing left but the skeletal remains of the man and woman and small child that she could identify as neither boy nor girl.

Cal spoke, his voice a choked whisper, "I'll see to the burying. You can ride off a ways if you like. It should be safe enough; it's been a good day since the Comanche hit. It was a small band, and if they're herding horses they won't be doubling back."

"I'll help," she said, dismounting and tying her mare to a broken-down corral fence.

Cal ferreted out two shovels from the lean-to behind the house, and an hour later, the grisly remains of the slaughtered ranch family were deposited in shallow graves next to the house. If relatives were found somewhere, they would be able to tell them where the bones of the ill-fated souls rested.

Cal and Danna had barely spoken since their arrival at the site of the massacre. Danna had not felt like talking. Somehow it seemed like a time for silence, but when Cal leaned his shovel against the adobe wall and strode around to the front of the house, it was like a signal that he had put it behind him. And he probably had, she thought. He had an unusual ability to do that. Was it a part of his performance? She did not know Cal Rivers that well yet, but she would.

"I'm going to go through the belongings that are left in the house," Cal said. "Maybe I can find out something about these people." He cast a glance skyward. "It'll be dark in a few hours. Do you want to spend the night here? The house can be straightened up. When I checked it earlier, it didn't look like the Comanche had even done much looting. They were apparently in a hurry and only stopped long enough for horses and scalps."

"No, I won't stay here, and I wish you wouldn't be so callous about this."

There were times when the man seemed devoid of emotion. Even now he did not respond to her anger.

"I won't be long," he said, as he turned into the house. "After we're finished here, we'd better head back to Pop's. They need to know what happened here. I don't think they're in real danger. They're not easy pickings like these folks were, but Pop can get word out to other families in the area to keep their eyes open. Some of the smaller farmers and ranchers move their families in to the Slash R for a spell when there are Comanche scares."

As she waited outside, she took off her hat and wiped the sweat off her brow with her forearm. She stood there, her eyes gazing out onto the vast, empty prairie for some minutes, before she surveyed the house, corrals, and few outbuildings, vacated now by the slain family and quickly becoming a part of the emptiness. Damn, she would be glad when she left this place. But unlike Cal Rivers, she would not be able to put this behind her any more than she had been able to put the rest of her past behind her.

This desolate ranch, the grotesque corpses, they were just more ghosts to haunt her.

14

DANNA REMEMBERED THE night that changed her life as if it had happened yesterday.

It was an uncommonly cool evening for south Texas in late June when Malcolm Sinclair pulled the buckboard into the Double Bar S ranch yard just before dusk. Danna could see him now: thick blond hair and mustache bleached nearly white by the Texas sun. She did not think of him as young then, but he would have been no more than thirty-five. She knew he was handsome—dashing she had heard a neighbor lady say. Standing nearly six foot two inches tall, the only flesh shrouding his bones was pure muscle, and she could see his pale blue eyes so placid and clear, like two mountain lakes, surveying the ranch in which he had invested ten years of his life and where he had buried two small sons younger than thirteen year-old Danna, both within five days after the diphtheria had struck. The pain was there buried deep within those eyes, but his spirit was unbroken. It was as if the ranch were a monument to that spirit, for the Sinclair homestead looked more appropriate for a Dutch farmer in New York than for the rugged rancher of the South Plains.

The yard was clean and tidy as a fastidious woman's parlor. The new frame house and barn and corrals, fresh-painted and shiny white. Malcolm Sinclair was generally a practical man, but he rejected a more functional abode for his family's dwelling and built a traditional Midwestern home, a gesture, Danna supposed, to his beloved Josephine—Jo, he called her—who was often homesick for the comfortable villages of her native Ohio.

Malcolm Sinclair pulled the wheel brake on the wagon and dropped the reins. Danna had been sitting with him on the wagon, resting her head against his powerful arm and dozing intermittently during the day's journey. She straightened and glanced over her shoulder where her mother slept on a blanket amidst the supplies and staples with year-old Timothy cradled in her arms, sucking vigorously at her small breast.

She turned to her father who had made no move to climb down from the wagon, his eyes slowly sweeping the ranch yard and back again as if he were trying to find something. His face revealed uneasiness, a look of puzzlement.

"What is it, Pap?" she asked, brushing a wisp of hair from her eyes.

He smiled reassuringly, revealing white, even teeth. "Nothing, honey, I guess. Nothing I can put my finger on." He climbed down from the wagon, still tossing his head nervously.

"Mama's plum tuckered out," Danna said, "and Timothy's hungry as a little pig. Mama said she's losing her milk."

Malcolm stood by the wagon box gazing sadly at his sleeping wife. "I know, honey. Your mama isn't doing so good. She wasn't cut out for the loneliness of this country. She's not like you and me. I told her I'd sell out and we'd move up north. I'd find something to do in town. But she wouldn't hear of that. She couldn't leave the boys, she said." He shook his head from side to side. "Nope, I guess she couldn't. When the chips are down, I don't know that I could, either. But your mama and me, we're staying for different reasons. She's staying to die; I'm staying to live." He picked up Danna. "Honeypot, remember something, don't ever do anything looking to die. Live your life."

Tears welled up in Danna's eyes, the green eyes that were her father's heritage. "Don't be sad, Pap, and don't worry about Mama. The trip to Dry Springs was just too much for her."

"Yeah, a day there and a day back is too far from the place for me, too, but we had to get supplies and your mama would have been scared to death to stay on the place without me here." He moved to the rear of the wagon to start unloading the supplies, and Danna crawled back into the wagon box to help.

"Shall I wake Mama?" she asked.

The voice that replied was not her father's mellow baritone. It was high-pitched and squeaky, like metal rubbing against glass.

"Don't make a move for your gun, mister, or you're a dead man."

Malcolm Sinclair froze a moment and then turned slowly toward the house. The door opened, and a man with a rifle in his hands leveled at Malcolm's mid-section stepped onto the porch. He was a slim man with long arms and legs that gave him a spider-like appearance. He wore moccasins and dirty buckskins. His face was dark, but he looked neither Indian nor Mexican, Danna thought, although he had a hawk-like nose and black shoulder length hair that was greasy and tangled. Her eyes darted from her father to the stranger and back again.

Josephine Sinclair began to stir and sat up in the wagon. Her eyes blinked with confusion. "What is it?" she asked.

"Just stay put, Jo," Malcolm said, unable to conceal the edge in his voice.

Josephine scooped up the baby and then saw the man. "Oh, my God," she gasped, "who—"

Malcolm interrupted. "What's your business, mister? This is our place. We're not looking for trouble."

Without taking his eyes off Malcolm, the intruder called, "You can come out now, boys. This feller don't want no trouble. Everything's settled."

Two more men emerged from the barn, and another one, a young Mexican, slipped from the house and joined his comrade on the porch. "Comancheros," Malcolm whispered. Shivers raced down Danna's spine and her heart began to pound in her chest. Comancheros. More than once she had heard the word that struck terror in the hearts of those who lived on the South Plains. Some were half-breeds, but many were Mexican or white. Their only allegiance was to gold and treasure to be harvested from the raiding, killing, and looting of Texas and New Mexican settlers and the illicit trading of plunder and people with the Comanche and, south of the border, Mexicans.

Malcolm inched closer to the wagon seat and the rifle that lay beneath.

The spider laughed. "Don't be stupid, mister. We know we can help ourselves to your supplies and every goddamned thing on your place, including your woman and little goldilocks, if it suits us."

Malcolm's face burst scarlet, and he took a step toward the spider before the Comanchero raced toward him and rammed the rifle barrel into his belly. "You ain't got no regard for the well-being of your little family here, mister, if you're going to cause a fuss. Next time you act like a jackass, Benito is going to blow the baby's brains to shit."

The Mexican's grip tightened on the handle of his revolver, and with a little flourish, he pointed it at Timothy. Josephine began to wail.

"You hold all the cards, mister," Malcolm said. "I'm listening."

The spider nodded with satisfaction. "I thought you looked like a man with sense. Now, you just do what we say and nobody gets hurt."

"Do I have your word on that?"

"My word!" The spider laughed again. "Why sure, you got my word. We just want to help ourselves to things and be on our way."

As Danna watched her father, she could see he was indecisive, uncertain. She had never seen him that way before, and it frightened her.

Josephine spoke for the first time. "Malcolm, for God's sake, do what they say, give them what they want. Please, Malcolm."

"Calm down, Jo. It's alright." His shoulders sagged, and Danna thought she could almost see the strength being sucked from his powerful body.

"Now," the spider said, "you just lay yourself down, face to the ground."

"Why? I won't cause any—"

"You giving me trouble, mister? I said so . . . that's enough."

Malcolm went down. "Spread eagle, mister." Malcolm obeyed. "There now, you're doing just fine." He stepped over toward the wagon. "Benny, look after the gentleman."

The Mexican's Navy Colt swept around, stopping when its barrel was aimed at the back of Malcolm Sinclair's skull. Danna saw the first faint traces of a smile on the Mexican's lips and she knew. She screamed just as he squeezed the trigger and the pistol roared and the bullet smashed into Malcolm's head. She saw her father's limbs flail, and then quiver for brief moments before he was still, and the sight of his face disappeared in a puddle of blood.

What happened next was a blur in Danna's mind. She could hear her mother's screams, rising in hysterical crescendo until they drowned out her own. She remembered Malcolm's Winchester appearing in her own hands, a gasping look of disbelief on the older man when he tried to wrest the rifle from her, and the bullet tore into his throat and left him bleeding on the ground like a slaughtered hog. There was the snarling face of a massive red-bearded man ascending upon her like a nightmarish monster as he snatched away the rifle and flung it across the yard, and then with equal ease threw her from the wagon seat.

Stunned and weak, she raised herself to her hands and knees before a hairy arm closed about her and lifted her up. She kicked and fought, clawed at his face like a ferocious cat, until his fist crashed into her cheek, knocking her half senseless. His hand grasped a hunk of her long hair and twisted it up in his hand like so much yarn until he held her like a puppet, balanced on numb legs, suspended by her own hair.

"Stinking bitch," he spat. "Now hold still and shut your mouth."

She was caught in his grip like a rabbit in a snare. Her father's words rung in her head. "Fight, Danna, fight for what's right. Fight for your life but know when to retreat and pull in your horns. Survive first, so you can live to fight another day. Give up a battle now and then to win the war."

She surrendered this battle to the red beard.

"Now, we understand each other," the red beard growled as she quit her struggle. Yanking her hair, he swung her around so that she faced away from him. "Now look at the fun your ma's having over there," he said. "You watch so you know what's expected of you."

Then through glazed eyes, she saw her mother on the ground, no more than five feet from Malcolm's still corpse, her frail white body stripped naked, half hidden by the spider who, with trousers wrapped about his ankles pumped frantically as Josephine gasped and sobbed almost inaudibly. Danna tried to pull away, go to her, but the red beard jerked her back brutally.

"Stay put, bitch, we're saving you for dessert."

Danna could do nothing but watch. The spider sighed, got up, and pulled up his trousers, his eyes fastened on Danna as he buckled his gun belt back on. "We should have killed her," he told the red beard, "for what she did to Harley."

"Shit," he replied, "Harley weren't no great loss. The old fart's time was about up anyway. The three of us have been doing the work and splitting up four ways. Besides, the Comanche like copper hairs. They'll pay a pretty price for this one."

"We're headed for Mexico."

"Then we can sell her to one of them Mexican whorehouses."

"I don't know," the spider said, noncommittally. "A kid that takes up a gun like that, she's more trouble than she's worth. I don't think she'll tame."

"I ain't seen a woman who can't be tamed," retorted the red beard. "Besides, I want to use her."

The spider walked behind them, and Danna could see the young Mexican man dropping his trousers and kneeling over Josephine who was unresisting.

"Who don't want to use her?" the spider said as he came close and jammed his hand down the blouse of her cotton dress and grabbed her breast.

She flinched, but tried to show no fear as his rough fingers twisted her nipple. He removed his hand and a sardonic smile curled on his lips.

"Plums, that's what they are. Little, juicy plums. Damned if she ain't taller than me, the gangly bitch. Older than she looks from a distance."

"Plenty old enough, that's for damn sure," the red beard said.

"There ain't one that ain't old enough for you," the spider said. "As far as you're concerned, you'd hump a baby if it was the only thing around."

Baby. Timothy. He wasn't crying. Where was he?

"I'm going to take her into the house," the red beard said. "I want to use her."

"Not now."

"But I want to," the red beard said, sounding like a little child.

"Later. We'll draw cards for who goes first. Use the woman; she's got about one more hump in her."

"My brother," Danna said, her voice surprisingly strong. "The baby. Where is he?"

"Want to see your brother, do you?" The spider's icy eyes bore into her own.

She did not challenge him, but neither did she avert his glare. "Yes."

"Say 'yes, sir,' and you can see your baby brother."

She hesitated. "Yes, sir."

He grabbed her by the wrist and pulled her away from the red beard and led her over to the wagon box. On the blanket, where an hour earlier he had nursed, securely and happily at his mother's breast, lay Timothy Sinclair, who Danna first thought was sleeping till she saw the awful depression on the right side of his skull where it had been caved in by a rifle butt. Her blood ran cold, her stomach churned like a Texas tornado, but she did not scream, and she did not cry. She was beyond that.

15

THE COMANCHEROS DECIDED to stay the night at the ranch. They had shut Danna in her parents' room. She sat at the side of the bed now, staring at the window that had been nailed shut by the red beard. If she broke the glass, they had warned, they would hear. She had thought it out: any attempt to escape now would be futile. She would not get through the broken window before they captured her, and she would pay. But the window glass gave her hope. She knew where she would go; she needed to get through that glass and a fifty yard head start, and they would never catch her. Not in a hundred years.

The night was clear and stars sprinkled the endless sky like glittering diamonds, causing a glow over the prairie that sifted through the window like a soft lamplight. The room was hot and stifling, closed off from the gentle breeze that kissed the rustling cottonwoods along the creek that meandered south from the house. As she studied and thought, she also listened to the voices of the men who played cards at the table outside the room. They made no effort to soften their voices, and their words floated easily through the door. She knew everything: what had happened and what was going to happen.

Another thing Malcolm had told her: use your brain, not your mouth, and you've got one up on the next guy. She knew their plans; they did not know hers. She was afraid, and she knew she should be devastated, reduced to whimpering servility. It occurred to her that her behavior was abnormal. She had not surrendered to her grief, and after all that happened, her mind was calculating and devious. Her mother was dead now, too. The red beard had cut her throat, she had heard him tell the others when he entered the house after having his turn with her. Poor Mama. But at least she was with Pap now. And Timothy. Or was she? Danna wondered. If Mama was right about her God, she would be in Heaven, but Pap never was much on God and the Bible, being more preoccupied with the here-and-now than the hereafter.

And poor Timothy. Mama always fretted because they had not been able to find a preacher to baptize him. He would go to Hell, she had said, because he had not been baptized. But what kind of a God, Danna thought, would send a little baby to Hell because his folks couldn't find a preacher? And what kind of a God could close his gates to a man like Pap? Mama would say that what had happened out there today was God's will. Bullshit, Pap would say. Those men had nothing to do with God.

Danna had to side with her father. God didn't send those Comancheros, and she didn't have any faith that God was going to get her away from these men. She was going to do that herself.

They were going to rape her, one by one, like they did with Mama. Their cards were going to decide who was first. She knew about rape, and she knew about sex and what men and women did with each other. Being raised on a ranch, she learned naturally how things worked with animals. She and her mother had been close until something snapped in Josephine's mind six months earlier, and her body began to slip, too.

Josephine had been a school teacher in Ohio, so she had taught Danna about life as well as books. Danna was a little vague about the specifics, but she had prepared herself mentally as well as she could for what was going to happen.

Suddenly, the men quit talking in the other room, and Danna heard footsteps outside her door. She stood and faced the door.

The red beard entered, staggering and obviously drunk. He told her that he had won her for the night and that she had to lie with him and do what he said or she would not see dawn. He ordered her to take off her clothes and she obeyed. He then grabbed her arm and roughly pulled her down on the bed with him, after which he promptly dropped off to sleep.

She lay beside him, still and unmoving, until he began to snore, and she saw the rhythmic rise and fall of his huge belly. Carefully, she eased herself off the bed and stood there a moment to be certain she had not disturbed him. Then she slipped into her bloomers and pulled on her dress. She would leave her shoes. They would be too noisy, and it would be too easy to track her. If only he had not left his gun in the other room.

How was she going to break the glass and get out the window before he caught her? She should have known they would not leave her alone in the room. She had anticipated them tying her up. The men had searched her parents' room for guns and ammunition and valuables, but they had not bothered with Malcolm's leather bag of possibles, tucked away in the corner of Josephine's oak chest. Danna had noticed, though, and she tiptoed to the chest and opened it quietly and removed her father's straight-edge razor from the bag. There was a way to slow the red beard down, stop him. She had helped her father butcher hogs and cattle and deer. The red beard reminded her of a fat hog. Perhaps if she thought of him that way—as a hog.

She crept softly back to the bedside and pulled the razor from its wooden handle. Beads of sweat erupted on her forehead. Could she do it? He did it to Mama, she had heard him brag. The image of the red beard using his knife on Josephine flashed through her mind. She did not hesitate.

She moved to him, pushed back his chin with one hand, and with the other, slashed the blade across his throat in a quick, single stroke. She felt the warm, thick blood in her hands even before she leaped away. She had felt the blade sever the thick tissue of his windpipe, and she had completed an arc that would have cut the vital arteries. She stood at the bedside as he struggled like a turtle on his back, choking and gurgling from his throat, as his hands clutched at his neck, trying to dam the raging river of blood that gushed there. He was unable to scream. He would be dead soon. His flesh was much softer than a hog's, she thought.

She scurried around to the other side of the bed and snatched up one of the red beard's boots. Then she took it and smashed the window pane with its heel. After clearing the jagged shards, she slipped easily through the window. She had escaped into the shadowy haven of the cottonwoods before a kerosene lamp illuminated the bedroom that had been her parents'.

She had her fifty yards head start.

16

CAL STOOD ON the platform near the front gate of the thick walls that surrounded the adobe hacienda and the compound of living quarters that included two large bunkhouses and a half dozen box-like residences that housed families of the foreman and top hands who called the Slash R home. His eyes were fixed on the horizon like a captain of a ship searching for an approaching gale. A dense cloud cover would blot out the stars tonight. It was dusty yet, and it would be a half hour before total darkness descended upon the ranch.

Cal scanned the corrals and barns and other outbuildings that lay outside the perimeter of the walls. There were several new lean-tos, he noted, constructed closer to the walls than some of the other buildings. The cedar poles that extended out from the structures to form the fence had the white shine of fresh hewn lumber. One pen for the bull, another for the five cows. They were expected in another month. A new breed Levi and Nate were experimenting with. Herefords. White-faces, Levi called them. Imports from England. They would be the first in the whole state, according to Levi, who had grudgingly conceded the idea was

Nate's. According to Nate, the new Hereford was a thickly muscled, meaty breed, and he wanted to try a cross with the Longhorns that were tough and resourceful, natural survivors, but were also lanky and boney and didn't produce that much meat on the bone. It sounded good, and with Levi's inborn instincts and Nate's educated judgment, Cal agreed that it was hard to see how the project could fail. As he surveyed the ever-expanding home ranch complex, Cal could see Nate's touches. There was a plan and purpose to the new construction, in contrast to the haphazard randomness of the original ranch complex.

He was glad for his older brother. Too often, strong men like Levi, well-meaning and good intentioned, dominated the son who stayed on the ranch, held on to the reins until the day they died, and then left something for the next generation to piss away. But if Levi did not let go of the reins, Nate would yank them away. He was not a man to spend a lifetime chasing his father's dreams. Nate had dreams of his own. His would be a building, growing generation. Levi would grumble and bitch about how Nate was getting too big for his britches and how he should never have given Nate so much authority or let loose of so much of his interest in the ranch, but Cal had a hunch that Nate would do the old man proud.

Anyway, if Levi and Aurelie Rivers had intended to raise their children to be a bunch of puppets, they had gone about it in the wrong way.

"Do you mind company?" It was Danna Sinclair's voice. She had scaled the ten-foot ladder when he turned and saw her. He reached out with his hand and helped her onto the board walkway.

"Your company's welcome," Cal said when she stood beside him. "It's not an evening for being alone."

"I know," she replied. "Cloudy, quiet, coyotes howling in the hills. It's easy to get a touch of melancholy on a night like this." She hesitated. "Those are coyotes I've been hearing, aren't they?" She ran her fingers carefully over the wicked shards of broken glass that were imbedded in the top of the adobe wall.

"Yes," he said, "just coyotes."

Her eyes studied the broken glass. "I've never seen this before," she said. "Broken glass used like this."

"You'll see a lot of it in Mexico," Cal said. "We broke a lot of bottles when I was younger to add this little touch. It was to discourage folks from climbing over. You'll notice in the daylight it goes about halfway down the outside wall. I guess it doesn't hurt, but it takes more than that to hold out Comanche or Apaches." He turned and looked out at the prairie. "We learned the hard way."

"What do you think, Cal? After what happened to the McKennas and now that ranch family near the Canadian . . . are the Comanche concentrating their raids in this part of the territory?"

"I wouldn't bet against it. Quanah's been working his way north again from all reports. For the moment, they seem to be striking only with raiding parties. The main band could be days, even weeks, behind. Mackenzie's been giving them hell in Texas; they could be looking for some mountain hideouts. Maybe as far west as the Sangre de Cristos. That would put the Slash R right in their path."

"But I had read that Mackenzie was badly wounded," Danna said. "There was speculation it would end his career."

"No, he's back in the field again. Has been since March." He had scouted for Mackenzie during the fall campaign.

"I've heard he's obsessed with killing Comanche. Almost insane with his crusade."

"Mackenzie's a mean, contrary bastard," Cal said. "I met him once at Fort Concho. He didn't look like any soldier I ever saw. He smelled like he hadn't had a bath since he came west. He had kind of a mangy, doggy look about him. You know, at first when I saw him I thought what I saw in his eyes was just plain craziness, like some bull that's got hold of some *loco* weed somewhere. But after talking to him, I decided that wasn't it. Mackenzie isn't so much crazy as he is stubborn. He doesn't know the meaning of quit. If the Kwahadi don't kill him, he'll chase them for the next twenty years if that's what it takes."

"But he's a good soldier?"

"Ranald Slidell Mackenzie is a crack Army officer. He was put in command of the 4th Cavalry in 1870 with broad authority to conduct a campaign against the Comanche in Texas. He was a colonel with a brilliant Civil War record. Grant called him the most promising young officer in the Army. Mackenzie was an unorthodox officer who fought the Comanche on their own terms. His enemies say he is arrogant and unapproachable. He has a reputation for being tough and merciless. He's decidedly not a book soldier; he's allowed his troopers to wear dirty uniforms and long hair. And he ordered them to get rid of their sabers, which he regarded as mere decorations and burdens. He molded a guerrilla-style force to combat the Indians under any conditions or terrain and weather."

"You seem to admire him," she observed.

"I respect the man, even though I think he's just a little short of crazy. For nearly two years Mackenzie hounded the Kwahadi. He set up patrols out of Forts Richardson, Griffin, and Concho and kept men in the field constantly. He had his victories, but he hasn't won the war . . . not yet."

"But he was wounded."

"Yeah, last fall he and his soldiers chased the Kwahadi into the Staked Plains. A murderous blizzard put an end to the chase but not before Mackenzie caught an arrow in the hip."

Cal continued, "Mackenzie won't have to wait twenty years, though. Maybe three years. Most of the other Comanche bands have already gone to the reservation. About all that are left are the Kwahadi and a few bands of Kiowas. Quanah's a smart man; he'll see the handwriting on the wall one of these days, and he'll make peace on some pretty good terms, I'd guess."

"You seem to respect Quanah, too."

"I do. From everything I've heard about him, he'd make a good lawyer but probably a better politician. I hope he can salvage some dignity for his people when it's over."

"You're very sympathetic for a man whose family has suffered at the hands of the Comanche the way you have and seen what they've done."

"I wasn't always so understanding. There was a time when all I wanted was to help Josh find the animals that killed Mom and Cassie and made off with Michael and make them pay five times over for what they'd done to my family. But in time I remembered that to the Comanche it was war. And there aren't any rules in war. God knows that the number of white women and children are only a few compared to the number of Comanche women and children that have been exterminated by the whites. And if Michael's out there alive somewhere, he's in more danger from his own people than he is from the Comanche." He rubbed his cheek thoughtfully. "On the other hand, maybe the Comanche are his people by this time."

Danna seemed pensive, engulfed by an aura of sadness. He decided to say nothing.

"You're right," she said, her eyes seemingly transfixed on some visage beyond the wall, lurking in the darkness that had swallowed them. "No, killing and mutilation are not unique to Comanche. I can testify to that."

"Death isn't a stranger to you," Cal said. "I could see that when we came upon that poor ranch family. You didn't run from what had to be done, but what you saw there was more than just murdered strangers."

"Murdered family," she said in a whisper, speaking more to herself than to Cal. "That's what I saw. Paps, Mama, Timmy—"

"Your family was murdered by Comanche?"

She turned her head toward him, and he saw a look of puzzlement in those wide green eyes that almost glowed in the dark. "I'm sorry, what did you say?"

"You said something about your family. I thought it had something to do with the Comanche."

"Comanche? No, not Comanche." She turned and took a few steps away from him.

Whatever it was, it was locked up inside of her, and she was not ready to let it out. Danna Sinclair was a very private woman, and she obviously bore scars from a life before Madison. And a female lawyer who ended up in a rough frontier town, several hundred miles from anything that could remotely be called civilization, had to have had a story to tell. But it was none of his damned business, and somehow the mystery of her past made her all the more alluring.

She was different than any woman he had ever met. Her

destiny was not tied to any man's. She had staked out her own. He had encountered women with more classical physical beauty, although not many. And there were many with greater seductive charm. But she had an independent mind, a fierce determination, a driving ambition that he supposed many men would find distasteful, if not intimidating. To Cal, these characteristics only made her more intriguing, more exciting, certainly no less feminine.

As they stood there silently on the parapet, he tried to call up memories of a dark, Spanish beauty he had once loved, but it was in vain. For the woman in his mind had green eyes and long strawberry-blonde hair that turned near copper in the full sun.

He tossed a look at Danna who was still turned away from him, leaning against the wall, staring into the darkness, apparently lost again in her thoughts. They were comfortable in each other's silence, and it was nice to enjoy someone's company without having to make conversation. Not many people would let you do that. Impulsively, he stepped closer to her.

"I've never met a woman like you."

Startled, she swung around to face him. She appeared slightly flustered. "A woman can take that any number of ways."

"It's a compliment."

Again she seemed uneasy about something. What the hell; he had nothing to lose. He took her in his arms and she didn't resist when his lips touched her own. For a moment, their kiss was soft and lingering, and he felt her melt against him, and he felt her fingers slip around his back. And suddenly, the gentleness in him gave way to the hunger that had gnawed at him, and desire surged in his loins and raced through his blood. He gripped her tightly, pressing his lips more intensely against hers.

He could feel the rapid rise and fall of her breasts against his chest, and he stroked her back and raked his fingers through her long hair. His hardness pushed through his trousers and against her abdomen. And he ached for her, wanted her. And that was all he could think about as his hand slipped to her thigh.

Suddenly, she tensed and stiffened, almost as if a knife had been stabbed into her back. She tried to pull away, but he persisted, and she seemed to panic and began to strike at him, almost hysterically, clawing him viciously. "No, no, no," she choked repeatedly. "No, no, no."

He released her, and she backed away, her eyes fixed challengingly on his like a cornered badger, fearing no man or animal, defying him to attack. She was crazed. He, too, took a step backward to signify he was no threat.

"I'm sorry," he said softly. "I wasn't trying to harm you. I don't understand."

She relaxed and the ferociousness evaporated. Tears welled up in her eyes and slowly, like two parallel streams, began to roll down her cheeks. "I'm sorry, too," she said, "and, no, of course, you don't understand."

He wanted to move to her again, take her in his arms, comfort her, but she was so damned unpredictable. How would she react? The decision was made for him when a thickly accented voice rose from the ranch yard below.

"Excuse me, *bitte* Cal, your *vader* says we should post watch this night. I *bin* first."

Cal looked down from the parapet at the unmistakable form of Hans Schmidt, a blond German with a close-cropped beard molded to his ruddy face.

He was a giant of a man, nearly six and a half feet tall, lean and rangy, like a Texas Longhorn, powerfully built with shoulders and biceps that looked like huge hams.

"It's all right," Cal replied. "Miss Sinclair and I were just getting ready to go in."

"*Sehr gut*," Schmidt said as he stepped onto the ladder.

As the man ascended, the lashed poles swayed and squeaked under his weight. He's a damn good man, Cal thought, as he watched him step onto the boardwalk. A few years older than himself, Schmidt was stubborn as a jackass but honest and unflinchingly loyal to Levi Rivers and the Slash R. He was a rampaging grizzly bear in the middle of a fight. Still, when Cal Rivers thought of Hans Schmidt, he thought of a gentleman. Men were not creatures of consistency. Nor women, he thought, cynically.

17

CAL LAY ON the bed with his fingers interlaced behind his head, staring at the ceiling as if he expected an explanation for his feelings to unfold there. He sighed deeply and rolled over on his side, facing the open window that pulled in a cool breeze this night, gazing vacantly at the darkness beyond.

The room was austere. It had a sanitized appearance. The bone-white walls were bare. This was a room he had shared with Josh as boys, but they had pretty much stripped it bare of their things when they left home and moved on to their separate lives. When Josh had returned for a time with Cassie, they had taken another room in the sprawling house, and this had one been set aside for Cal's occasional stops at home. Yes, he thought, this place was home, and perhaps someday he'd carve out a niche there.

Tonight, though, it was not thoughts of the future refusing to let him drift away in the mercy of sleep. It was a young woman with the red-gold hair and fathomless, jade eyes. He had not known her for more than a short time, but somehow she had worked her way into his head, shattered his concentration and addled his brain. He must remember they had a task in Santa Fe and shared a mission that would, hopefully, soon be over.

Damn, he had really lost his head, behaved like a clumsy, over-anxious kid on a first trip into a whore's bed. Had he just imagined that she wanted him, too? He gingerly poked the sore and swollen scratch marks she had left on his neck. Why had she reacted so violently? Crazy as he had been, he would never have taken her against her will. Never. Surely she must have known that.

Suddenly, there was a soft rapping at his bedroom door, and reflexively he reached down and pulled the sheet over his naked hips. "Who is it?"

"It's Danna." Her voice was soft, hesitant. "May I come in?"

"Yes, of course," Cal said, "come in." He reached over and turned up the flame in the oil lamp as the door opened, and Danna stepped into the room. She closed the door behind her and stood there for some moments, her eyes casting about the room, strangely, almost fearfully, as if she had just walked into a grizzly's den. This was twice in the time he had known her, the second time tonight, that she had shown anything close to insecurity. Until tonight, he had known her as a confident, intelligent, hard-headed professional. Gentle, on occasion; feminine, always. But afraid? Never.

"Danna?"

She did not reply but stepped quickly to the foot of his bed and stood there for some moments, her eyes still jumping nervously from wall to wall.

Then her gaze fastened on Cal. "You don't know how difficult it was for me to come here." Her throaty whisper was barely audible, and her lips trembled as she spoke. "I don't know if I'm going to be very good at this."

She slipped off her robe, and he pulled back the sheet, sharing her nakedness, as she slipped into the bed beside him. This time he was patient, almost deliberate as he took her in his arms, tendered soft kisses, and gently caressed and stroked before they finally coupled.

And he found her to be very good at this.

18

It was nearly dusk of the second day following their capture by the Comanche when Josh caught sight of telltale streams of campfire smoke that seemed to be rising from nowhere on the horizon. It had been a grueling ride at Comanche breakneck pace. With hands bound behind his back, he had fought an unending battle to stay in the saddle. He had not had a chance to speak with Jessica Chandler since their capture because the Comanche had taken care to keep them separated, even when they camped the night in a grove of pecan trees. None of the Comanche spoke English, or if so, did not admit to it, and they had communicated their wishes by the occasional grunts and shoves and sign language.

Josh rode behind Quanah Parker and a squat Indian with mahogany brown skin, who appeared to be a lesser chief of some kind, and Jessica trailed along behind with three or four of the some twenty warriors. He glanced over his shoulder and noticed, as usual, that Jessica was holding up gamely. With disheveled hair and a dust-caked, wind-burned face, she looked much like she had at their first meeting, but she sat straight in the saddle with her proud head uplifted, refusing to display the fear that she no doubt felt.

But she was unharmed. That was what puzzled Josh. By all odds, Jessica Chandler should have been raped many times over by now and her scalp of beautiful raven hair hanging from some Comanche's belt. There was a chance she had been claimed by some warrior as a potential slave or wife. She had shown the good sense not to be a troublemaker and had endured the journey without slowing the progress of the war party. Unlikely as her survival was, it could be explained.

But it was not so easy to account for the sparing of his own life. Comanche, perhaps more than any Plains tribe, abducted white children and raised the more promising captives as their own. And, of course, an occasional woman was accepted into the camp. But a white male? Unlikely.

Why had they not mutilated him, killed him, in the ash grove where they had been captured? He could only conclude that they were saving him for tribal entertainment. He shook off the thoughts of what could lie ahead for him and reminded himself that he was alive. He had wanted to locate the Kwahadi encampment and arrange a parley. Well, he had found the Kwahadi all right: the herd stallion, himself. Now if they would only give him a chance to talk.

As they drew nearer the smoke, the Comanche ponies slowed to a steady walk till they came to the edge of a vast chasm. Nearly a thousand feet below, stretching along both sides of a serpentine ribbon of creek, were seemingly endless clusters of tipis. It was a sprawling encampment, larger than any he had ever imagined, much less seen. If the McKenna girl was alive, she was here. If Michael Levi Rivers was alive, he was here.

The war party dismounted and Josh was pulled harshly from his saddle and his bonds released. In a few moments, as they led their horses over the narrow and treacherous trail that zigzagged its way down the sheer wall, Josh understood why. His only way out was over the edge of the escarpment and into the abyss that ended in rocks below.

An hour later, Josh sat alone on a matted buffalo robe in one of the tipis that covered the canyon floor. Although it was well past sundown now, the canyon was strangely illuminated by a moon that seemed cast in silver and a spray of starlight that reflected off the slate white canyon walls. Enough light sifted through the openings of the tipi to permit Josh to appraise his buffalo hide jail.

It was evident that no one else occupied the tipi, for there were no furnishings beyond the several buffalo robes. The tipi was cool and the air fresh, and Josh saw that the tipi walls had not been drawn completely to the ground, leaving an air space of several inches all around. The space, together with the smoke hole near the top, provided excellent ventilation. Cal had told Josh once, compared to a good tipi, the best white man's lodging was poor makeshift.

Suddenly the stiff pelt that covered the three foot high entry opening was pulled aside, and a young woman with long, sable hair, and wearing a soft buckskin dress, stepped in with a large, envelope-like parfleche bag in her hand. She knelt in front of him, and when the milky light that streamed through the smoke hole illuminated her face, he saw an extraordinarily beautiful Comanche woman. As she raised the fold-over flap of the bag and removed a bulging, elongated object, she spoke softly in perfectly enunciated English. "Quanah says you are to eat. He will speak with you when the sun rises." With her teeth, she tore open the sausage-like object in her hands, peeled back its covering, and placed it on the robe in front of Josh.

"Pemmican," she said. "Hunting has not been good."

"Thank you," Josh said as he reached into the moist, sticky mixture. "Are you permitted to stay with me?"

"Until you are finished eating."

"Then I'll eat slowly." Sucking the pemmican from his fingers, he savored its rich sweetness. He had not eaten since morning, and only now did the hunger pains start to slice at his stomach. He supposed that the assurance of at least a short reprieve to state his case had released his mind to thoughts of something other than survival.

He had tasted pemmican before. Most whites called it "Indian bread" since the Comanche had no bread, and this was the closest substitute. In fact, it was a mixture of wild berries, cherries or plums, mashed and partially dried in the sun, often including walnuts or pecans, before being mixed with meat, which was pounded thoroughly and softened over a fire before tallow and marrow fat were added. The mixture was often stored in buffalo paunches or large intestines, which had probably been no more than partially cleaned. Josh had found it delicious when sliced and dipped in honey, and he had no complaints now. He knew without the woman saying so that food must be scarce, for pemmican, which could be stored for years, was generally not eaten by the Plains Indians when other foods were available.

After greedily devouring several handfuls of the mixture, as the woman watched him with keen interest, he spoke. "It is very good. I was nearly starved. We had only a few wild berries for breakfast. Nothing for dinner."

"Comanche have no such meal times," she said. "If there is food in the village and they are hungry, they eat. In times like these, when there is little food, they eat less often. Perhaps not for two or three or more days."

Josh decided he did not have time to linger on amenities. "There was a woman with me. Where is she?"

"She is not being harmed. Leaping Antelope has claimed her. If she works hard and does as she is told, she may become his third wife."

As Josh's eyes adjusted to the dusky light of the tipi, he wondered if the woman was a half-blood. She had dark eyes of indefinable color, but her skin was lighter hued than most full-blood Comanche. And there was the matter of her fluency in his language. She could have learned English from a white mother, he supposed, but he doubted that would have been approved by the tribe's elders. He judged her to be perhaps twenty to twenty-five years of age, average height for a white woman, but taller than most Comanche squaws. She was slender and willowy.

He took a chance. "I don't think you are Comanche," he said.

"I have been Comanche for nearly eight years when the leaves fall. I was fourteen summers old when I became a Comanche."

"My name's Josh Rivers. What's your name?"

"Yes, I know who you are, Mr. Rivers." She paused meaningfully, as if giving him a chance for her words to sink in. The fact that she knew his name had caught him by surprise, but he did not pursue it for the moment.

She continued, "I am called 'She Who Speaks.'"

She was aptly named, Josh thought. There was no doubt a reason beyond coincidence. "But your other name . . . the one you had before your capture."

"I am no captive, Mr. Rivers, and consider that if you should be so fortunate as to depart this village, you would feel obliged to inform the Army of my name. The soldiers would notify others and raise false hopes that would only be dashed when I did not return. Therefore, I had no name . . . no life . . . before I became Comanche. I am She Who Speaks, wife of Four Eagles, mother of a strong Comanche son, a woman who may speak in Kwahadi councils."

Her face was solemn as she spoke, her words matter-of-fact and firm, not boastful. He should have known she was a woman of some rank, a rarity, if not an oddity, among the Comanche. An ordinary squaw, least of all a white captive, would never have been permitted such time alone with him. Certainly she would have not been so free and confident in her conversation. This young woman had the implicit trust of her tribesmen. She was not there to perform the servile task of dispensing nourishment to a prisoner. And she knew his name. She was charged with a mission.

He did not think she was taking him for a fool. She was probably being intentionally evasive, like an Indian, which he guessed she was in all the ways that count. She was being subtle, a bit taunting, playing little games in her approach. He made a point of shifting his attention to his attack on the tasty pemmican.

Only after he had eaten his fill did he look up and meet her eyes again. "Some water would be nice." Her face did not change expression, but he thought he caught a glint of laughter in her eyes before she rose quietly, gracefully, like a mountain cat, and left the tipi. In a few moments, she returned with a paunch of water.

She sat down, and again he could feel her eyes studying him while he gulped down more water than good sense dictated. Then handing the paunch back to her, he said, "Thank you. Now, maybe you'd like to tell me what you really came here to talk about." Again he saw the glint in her eyes that said she knew he was onto her little game.

"I speak for Quanah."

"You're his messenger?"

"Yes, and interpreter. I am with him always when the Comancheros come to trade or when other friendly whites are admitted to our village."

She was powerful. A woman in her position would have great influence if she did not abuse it. And she apparently had not, for it would not have been tolerated long in the Comanche male-dominated society. It also explained why she spoke such good English. She was obviously a woman of some education and breeding, but she had had the opportunity to hone the language of her white origins. In fact, she had evidently made sort of a profession of it. Many young captives, after a number of years, forgot their first language. Cynthia Ann Parker, Quanah's mother, nine years old when she was abducted from her family's stockade in east central Texas, could not speak a word of English when she was recovered against her will twenty-four years later.

"Why can I not speak with Quanah?" Josh asked. He was reluctant to show his cards until he was face to face with the famous war chief.

"Quanah has said I should decide if he will speak with you in the morning. If you do not wish to talk with me now, I shall do what I must."

The implication was clear that she was not going to put in a good word with Quanah if Josh did not state his purpose here and now.

"How do you know I have words for Quanah? He found me;

what makes you think I was looking for him?"

"Quanah knows," she said mysteriously. Then she shifted as if to rise and leave. "But if you do not—"

She would have made a good poker player, too. "I do," he said.

She sat back down on the buffalo robe.

"I'm looking for someone . . . a young woman. Her name is Erin McKenna. She would have been captured in a raid near Madison in New Mexico territory about a year ago, north and west of what the white men call the Cimarron Cutoff. You would know her by her hair. It's red. Very red, I am told."

She Who Speaks betrayed nothing. "And what makes you think Quanah would surrender such a young woman even if she was in our camp . . . which she is not."

"Your people need food and goods they can acquire from the Mexicans or Comancheros. The McKenna girl is wealthy. I can arrange for payment in gold that will allow them to buy cattle from the Mexicans."

"We can take cattle when we choose."

"Not as many as you need; not with the Army hunting you."

"How do we know that you would not be working with the Army?"

"My word. And I can provide you with other assurances. The exchange could be made when the gold is delivered. But if this worries you, I can provide money. I know you have ways of buying what you need."

"We are told that Joshua Rivers is a lawyer and that his brother rides with the soldiers. How are we to believe that you were not sent by the soldiers?"

"My brother no longer scouts for the Army, and as a lawyer, I speak for my client, Erin McKenna's aunt. My responsibility is to her, no other. As a lawyer, that is my obligation. You're not so long removed from the white man's world you wouldn't know that. You can explain to Quanah."

"It does not matter. This girl that you speak of . . . she is not here. She was not taken by the Kwahadi. But I will be able to let you speak with Quanah . . . perhaps. Do you have more to say?"

He sat there, meeting the even gaze of her eyes, agonizing for some moments. Should he ask for Michael? She would admit nothing, of course, but he might catch her off guard, see something in her face that would tell him his son was alive and in the Kwahadi camp. He decided against it. It was unlikely that he would learn anything from this shrewd woman, and he might learn more if he kept quiet for the time being. Besides, he was taking a damn big bite to seek the release of one captive. To ask for two might seem like gluttony and could jeopardize the release of both. The chance that Michael, nursing at his mother's breast when he was taken, being alive and in this particular village were just too remote for him to take any gamble that might interfere with the purchase of Erin McKenna's freedom. And as much as it hurt, his duty was to her right now.

"Only one thing," Josh said.

"What is it?"

"I have never seen so many tipis in one place. Too many for just Kwahadi. Are there other Comanche bands here?"

"Yes."

"Kiowa and Cheyenne? What are they doing here?"

Her stoic face cracked with a sardonic smile. "You are a lawyer who asks questions when he should be answering them. I do not think you are as wise as we have been told." In a single fluid motion, she rose and disappeared through the opening of the tipi.

Josh lay back on the buffalo robe, determined to get the sleep he would surely need the next morning. Before he drifted into a troubled and uneasy sleep, again and again, his mind turned over the conversation he had with She Who Speaks. They knew his name; they knew he was a lawyer. She had intimated that they knew other things. He had said nothing to Jessica Chandler, so they could not have gotten the information from her. How? Who?

19

WHEN JOSH PULLED back the tipi's hide door flap, the glare of the fiery morning sun blinded him momentarily. He remembered that Cal had told him once that the Comanche always positioned their lodges so they opened to the rising eastern sun. As his eyes adjusted to the light, he noticed that no guards seemed to be posted near the tipi, not that it would have made any difference. The canyon itself was a natural prison, and the chances of a lone white man slipping away from the Indians that covered the chasm floor like a swarm of bees were less than slim.

The canyon was alive. Squaws were busying themselves with camp chores and the fires. Half naked children raced through the village. He crawled through the opening and then stood outside the tipi for some minutes surveying the morning activities of the encampment. Josh knew that the Comanche referred to themselves as "the People." To many white men, they were far from human, closer to animals.

Josh had never shared that opinion, not even in those bleak days following his mother's and Cassie's deaths and Michael's abduction. It would be hard for any man to deny their humanness,

Josh thought, if he could see them now, working and playing in the tranquil security of their village. Josh was struck with the thought that the scene upon which he gazed was showing him a loving, gentle side of the Comanche that he had never considered before, much less seen.

Remembering the commotion their arrival had caused in the village the day before, he had expected that his appearance would attract some attention. On the contrary, he had earned no more than disinterested glances from several of the squaws. The Indians seemed otherwise oblivious to his presence.

Well, he couldn't wait any longer. His bladder felt like it was swollen to the size of the paunch he had drunk from the night before, and he was going to have to do something about it. Trying to appear casual and nonchalant, he strolled through the village, working his way to the edge of the encampment, and when he had gone no more than twenty-five feet outside the perimeter of the camp, he came upon the scattered heaps of human dung that told him he had located the place he was looking for.

He was standing there, facing away from the camp, relieving himself when he heard the familiar voice behind him. "You are to come with me, Rivers." He was startled at the sound of her voice. Then she added impishly, "You may finish making your water, if you wish."

20

JOSH HAD AN idea of how it must feel to face a jury without a lawyer, as he sat in Quanah Parker's expansive tipi, facing the sober faces and appraising glares of Quanah and the four Comanche he guessed were either members of Quanah's counsel or chiefs of the other bands that were camped in the seemingly endless canyon. She Who Speaks sat at Josh's side, but if she was a spokesman for anyone, it was Quanah, and he would have no way of knowing whether she conveyed his words accurately to the great war chief.

He met the gaze of Quanah's gray-blue eyes unflinchingly. The Comanche did not seem nearly so fierce without his war paint, however his bearing on the tipi floor, as on the back of his huge stallion, was stately and regal. Even though he was dressed in a simple buckskin war shirt and breechclout, his only concession to vanity was the long braids of gleaming walnut-brown hair wrapped in otter fur and a wide, beaded choker that graced his neck. The other Comanche were more elaborately attired, several wearing leggings decorated with ornate, intricate beadwork, draped with cone-shaped bells and eagle feathers plaited in their hair.

But there was no doubt that Quanah, less than thirty years of age and by far the youngest, was the leader.

They sat there in silence before Quanah spoke at some length in Comanche dialect to She Who Speaks, all the while keeping his eyes fastened on Josh.

She Who Speaks translated. "Quanah wishes to know what you will trade for the flame-haired girl you speak of."

"Then she is here?"

"She might be. But what would you trade for her if she was found?"

Josh decided he would save time by finding out what the Comanche chief wanted. "Tell Quanah to name his price. If it is fair, I will meet it."

Quanah and She Who Speaks engaged in an extended dialogue before she spoke again. "Another has offered Quanah five thousand dollars American money in gold and one hundred new rifles the whites call Winchesters."

"For Erin McKenna?"

"Yes."

"Who has made this offer?"

"A Comanchero. More cannot be said. He will no doubt take her to Mexico where she will be sold as a whore."

Not at that price, Josh thought. Somebody else is trying to ransom Erin McKenna but not to bring her back to claim her rightful inheritance. The Comanchero was bearing a death warrant, probably signed and sealed by Oliver McKenna.

"Six thousand dollars," Josh said. "No rifles."

They had Erin McKenna, of course, and apparently she was for sale. He was close to accomplishing his mission, closer than he ever hoped to get.

Quanah's response was not surprising. He spat it out, anger flashing in his stormy eyes.

"Fifty rifles," She Who Speaks said.

Josh said, "No, I cannot provide the rifles. That would be breaking the laws of my people and my own code. Ask Quanah if he can understand that. Would he wish to deal with another Comanche who could not keep the laws of his band?"

Quanah appeared thoughtful as She Who Speaks translated. He responded in brief words that sounded more like a command than a reply. "He will talk no more this day," She Who Speaks said. "You are to leave."

"But I . . . I need an answer quickly."

"It would be wise to do as he says. Leave. You will be treated as a guest in his village; you will eat at any fire that suits you. But do not stray from the Kwahadi camps. Others may not deal so generously with you."

Her voice was strained as though she were trying to communicate to him the importance of his prompt obedience. He rose and left the tipi. As he walked away, wandering aimlessly through the village, he tried to draw some conclusions from his brief, unsatisfactory encounter with Quanah Parker. She Who Speaks probably had been evasive. If the McKenna girl was in the village, she was hidden or they would not have given him the run of it. She could be with one of the other bands whose villages were strung along the banks of the shallow creek that split the canyon floor.

Quanah clearly had the authority to negotiate for her ransom, so it was obviously under Kwahadi control.

The rifles. If he could only offer the rifles. But he had taken an oath to uphold the law, and he had not taken it casually. And how could he provide the weapons when he knew they would immediately be turned upon settler families like his own?

And what about Michael? Josh would keep his eyes open. Was it just unquenchable hope that gnawed at him, or did he actually feel the presence of little Michael Rivers, the son he hardly knew, in the winds that swept through the canyon walls?

He spent the day wandering around the camp. He watched for some sign of Jessica's whereabouts and worried about her fate. He stopped at the fires of several families and shared in their meals, eating sparingly, because he could see that food supplies were severely limited—mostly pemmican and beef or bison jerky. At dusk he retired to his own lodge, deciding he should grab what rest he could to prepare for whatever ordeals might lie ahead.

Just as Josh was reaching for the buffalo robes on his tipi floor to form a softer bed, She Who Speaks appeared as suddenly and quietly as a ghostly visage in the doorway of the lodge. "I am to speak with you," she announced.

"Good," Josh said, gesturing for her to sit with him on one of the robes. "I had about given up hope of hearing from you today."

"Have you eaten?" she asked.

"Yes, I did as you suggested. I sat down at the fires of those who were eating. Your people fed me whatever they had. I wish other whites could see this side of the Comanche. Perhaps the killing wouldn't come so easily. But perhaps the Comanche should see other sides of the whites, as well. I wonder . . . does anyone ever win a war? Yet, there are things worth fighting for."

"How do men of peace resolve these things?"

"It's a damn tough question; nobody's answered it yet. I suppose they never will." He grinned sheepishly. "You'll have to forgive me. I haven't had anyone to talk to, and I guess I'm making up for lost time." For the first time, he caught the faint trace of a smile on her lips, and there was warmth in her eyes he found encouraging.

"I think maybe Quanah is right after all," she said. "Perhaps you are the one."

"I don't understand."

She did not explain. "We shall discuss the price for the girl. Quanah will agree to your offer, if you will include twenty-five of the new rifles."

"No, there cannot be any rifles."

"Then the girl will be sold to the Comanchero."

"The Comanchero will kill her. He has been hired by the girl's uncle who stands to gain great wealth by her death. Quanah would be foolish to sell to the Comanchero. We will pay just as much or more as he can; we just cannot provide the rifles. If the guns are so important to Quanah, he can get them from someone else . . . exchange the gold dollars for them. If the girl is returned to me, she will be returned to her people alive and well. It might be taken as a token of goodwill. Quanah will need that soon. He is no fool, and neither am I, so why don't you tell me what Quanah really wants . . . why he chose to let me live."

She was silent for some moments and her eyes narrowed as though she were on the verge of an important decision.

"Quanah wishes for you to be his lawyer."

Josh smiled. "As near as I can see, Quanah is the law around here. Why would he need a lawyer?"

"It is finished. Bad Hand Mackenzie will not rest until the last Comanche is dead or on the reservation. Quanah wishes you to speak for him, to negotiate terms most favorable for our people.

Afterward, he will still be Comanche, but he will learn the white man's ways. He will lead the people in peace as he has in war. To do this, he will need the help of white men he can trust. He will need lawyers to guard him against the treachery of the white man's papers. Already the whites call him by the name of his mother's people . . . Parker. He will be known as Quanah Parker."

Josh could not believe what he was hearing: a Comanche chief trying to retain him as a lawyer. "Tell me more about what Quanah has in mind."

"You will be his lawyer?"

"If I can see where I might be helpful in negotiating terms, and if certain conditions are satisfied, I will consider it. Also, I must know what Quanah expects of me before I can say."

"Can I speak with your promise that my words will never be repeated outside this of this tipi if you should decide you will not be the lawyer for the People?"

"Yes."

"If Quanah surrenders without terms, he and the chiefs will go to prison. The People will be left without leaders, and they will be herded to the reservations like lowly sheep. Quanah will make peace if he and the chiefs will be allowed to remain with the People. And the Kwahadi must be given land and cattle with which to start a new life. You are to secretly contact the authorities, dealing only with those you decide can be trusted. Quanah knows this will take time, perhaps a year or more, but it must be done in a way so the whites do not know the weakness of our position."

Damn. If they decided he could not be trusted, he would not leave the village before his throat was cut and his balls stuffed in his mouth. "It would be a great honor and a greater challenge,"

Josh said, "to be a part of something that would bring about a lasting peace between the whites and the Comanche."

"You would be paid as Quanah's lawyer. You would be paid very well. That is how it is done, is it not?"

"That is how it is done."

She continued, "No others in our band know of Quanah's plans—neither do the chiefs of the other bands and tribes camped here. Quanah will not betray them; they will do as they see fit. Quanah speaks only for the Kwahadi that choose to follow him, but I can tell you that when the time comes, all will follow."

"I will do it," Josh said. "As I said before, conditions must be met."

"And what are those conditions?"

"The return of the McKenna girl."

"It will be arranged. Of course, we must still be paid the six thousand dollars in gold."

They drove a damned hard bargain. Josh wasn't all that sure that Quanah Parker needed a lawyer. "Yes, the gold bullion will be delivered to a place you designate. But there are other conditions. The woman who was with me must be permitted to leave also."

"But she has been claimed as a wife."

"She has been here only a few days. For the price of a few ponies the warrior will recover from his loss. You cannot tell me that Quanah has so little influence he can't get the woman released."

"It will be done," She Who Speaks said.

Josh could sense her irritation, and debated whether to present his final condition. Was he letting his personal concerns cloud his professional judgment? Probably. But he could not live with himself if he did not try.

"A final condition," he said.

She eyed him suspiciously. "You are being unreasonable. You have made too many conditions."

"This is the last. My son. I want my son returned to me."

Her answer came too quickly to suit him. "We know nothing of your son. We cannot return what we do not have. It cannot be done." Her voice was firm. "We cannot satisfy this last condition any more than you can provide the rifles. If you will not be our lawyer, then the girl will be traded to the Comanchero."

He did not know if she was lying. Perhaps she did not even know one way or the other. If Michael were alive, he would be a Comanche now. Such children were loved dearly by their parents and not easily surrendered. Quanah would know, too, that the possibility of Michael's presence in the village would be good insurance in case the lawyer was not as trustworthy as they had judged him to be. As much as it hurt him to draw back, he knew this was not the time to press the issue. If he worked with Quanah and the Kwahadi, there would be other opportunities. At this point, he had everything to lose and nothing to gain by not striking a bargain with Quanah.

"You win," Josh said. "I withdraw my condition. I will speak for Quanah at the white councils as he wishes, and I will deliver the ransom. But I need proof that Erin McKenna lives."

“The woman you were naked with can verify.”

He felt she was having fun at his expense now.

"Quanah will speak with you again when the sun rises," She Who Speaks said. "I will tell you now that he is learning the English language. He understands much of what you say, but he will not speak until he is comfortable with the tongue."

21

DANNA SAT BEHIND the warped, wobbly desk that George Hatter had installed in the vacant office across the hall from Josh's. She had no complaints about the room. Its white plastered walls were as clean as bleached lime, and the wide uncurtained window opened onto the plaza. But the only furnishings were the desk that had evidently been run over by a team of horses at one time or another and two very uncomfortable straight backed chairs, one of which accommodated her sore bottom.

The law clerk had not been pleased to receive the letter of introduction Josh sent with her, and he had obviously been horrified at the prospect that she would plant herself in Josh's office in his absence. Mr. Hatter had been irritatingly formal and excessively polite during the two weeks she had been in the office. She did not think he disliked her so much as he resented her intrusion into his domain. Getting information from him was like tearing a bone away from a feisty dog. In his clerkish way, she supposed he did maintain a certain order in the office, although she found herself growing increasingly impatient with his mechanical, plodding way of doing things.

Fortunately, Linda de la Cruz was Hatter's opposite: quick wit, a sense of humor and pretty much unflappable. Their personalities meshed. Linda's fluency in both Spanish and English, and passable knowledge of Pueblo, made her invaluable to the office, and she was a magician on a brand new machine Josh had purchased from E. Remington & Sons, a gun manufacturer. It was called the typewriter, and the typist could quickly print clean, legible letters on a sheet of paper. To Danna's delight, Linda was teaching her to use the machine. When it gained general acceptance, Danna thought, it would revolutionize the legal profession's way of doing things.

There was nothing old-fashioned about Josh Rivers's approach to his law practice; she would give him credit for that. She chastised him mentally, though, for the way he neglected his business. He was, no doubt, an excellent lawyer, and this accounted for why he had so much work. But there was enough business for three lawyers in the office, and she faulted him for not either turning away the work or bringing additional lawyers into his firm. Clients deserved better treatment, and if he had had to scratch out a living the way she had, he would be more appreciative of that fact. She had been swamped from the moment she walked into the office, putting out fires that should have been doused by Josh Rivers weeks ago. She had not even had time to properly prepare for the critical hearing she faced the next day on the McKenna case, and she knew she would be working far into the night.

Even now as the sun crawled behind the Sangre de Cristo Mountains, and the shadow cast by the Palace of Governors across the plaza faded into grayness, she had yet another of Josh's clients to see and to pacify. She sighed, set aside the crisp sheets of paper she had been writing on, and rose from the chair and walked out into the outer office. Linda de la Cruz sat at the typewriter, her fingers dancing over its keys as she finished the will Danna had drafted that afternoon. She was glad to see that George Hatter had left for the day. He had a habit of waiting around with a disapproving scowl on his face until the last person left the office.

"Linda, there's no hurry about the will," Danna said. "Why don't you finish it in the morning?"

Linda looked up, her dark eyes as sparkling and bright as they had been when the office opened that morning, smiled warmly, revealing teeth that were white, even pearls against the backdrop of dark, sleek skin. "I am almost finished, Miss Sin . . . Danna," she replied. She nodded toward the typewriter. "Josh said this was a toy he was purchasing for me. It truly is a delightful toy."

"Well," Danna said, "it's also a very practical one. I would rather think of it as a valuable tool. Anyway, leave whenever you wish. I'll be here quite late, I'm afraid."

"I have no plans this evening. Can I be of any help?"

"No, but thank you, Linda. I'm at a point where I'm the only one who can do anything about this case." Then she saw the face of the tight-lipped, graying man who glared at her with smoldering eyes from across the room. "You must be Mr. Pierce," she said moving toward him with her hand extended.

He stood up and hesitated as though suspicious of her hand before accepting it with a calloused grip that was firm, yet somehow cold.

"Won't you come into my office?" Danna said. "I'll see if I can be of any help."

He grunted something unintelligible, but he followed her. When they were seated in the austere room, he cast his eyes about uneasily as if he were sorry he had ever come there. She could tell he would be a hard one to win over. But she knew also that while her femaleness might be a slight handicap with him, Westerners, more than any other breed, were more concerned with what you could do than who you were. Race or religion or gender were abstract and superficial prejudices to men like this one; biases were quickly tossed aside if you could do the job that needed doing. For a saloon girl, that job was a pretty smile, batting eyelids, voluptuous breasts. For a lawyer, it was clear thinking and sound advice.

"I'm sorry Josh isn't here, Mr. Pierce," she said. "He's away on a very important case. Mr. Hatter told me you have some problems concerning your ranching operation that require immediate attention. I'll try to help you if I can."

"Yes, ma'am. I have some legal business that needs to get done *pronto* or I ain't going to be ranching much longer. I don't know how much you know about my predicament."

"Well, I think I can save us some time, Mr. Pierce. Josh's notes tell me that you own close to 25,000 acres of land, some of it lush grazing in the mountain valleys southwest of Taos. But you don't own enough cattle to fill a quarter of it, and you can't stock the ranch because you're short of cash. You've reached the limit of credit at the banks. In terms of net assets, some people might say you're a wealthy man. But it appears to me, Mr. Pierce, that you're what some folks call 'land poor.'"

Enoch Pierce's eyes grew intense as she spoke, and she thought she saw less hostility in his grim, weathered face. "You don't exactly coat your words with sugar, ma'am, but I think maybe you and me can do business. I sure as hell need cash, all right, and I could get some easy enough. I got two or three neighbors just itching to take some of my prime grazing land off of my hands. They'd pay dear for it, and I could walk away with half my land free and clear along with the cattle to stock it and money in the bank."

"Selling off that land," Danna said, "would be harder than taking off an arm or leg. It's part of you and you're part of it."

He sighed and slumped back in his chair. "Not many folks understand that, ma'am. You must know something about my breed."

"Yes, I think so, Mr. Pierce. My father was one of your breed. Now, tell me, did Josh make any recommendations the last time you met?"

"Nope. I was to come back in two or three days. Well, I did, and Josh was gone again."

"He had a few words written at the end of his notes, Mr. Pierce. Corporation. Pierce Land & Cattle Co. I think he had in mind that you would set up a corporation for your ranching operation. Do you understand how that might work?"

"Sort of. It's not too clear in my head. It means I'd have to let some other folks in on my ranch."

"In a manner of speaking, yes. There is a lot of eastern money available these days, Mr. Pierce, but not for loan. The men that have it want more than interest. They want to speculate on the future of the West. They think land is going to become more valuable . . . that the cattle industry has a boundless future. They'd rather own a part of that future than have the interest now."

"Now that you mention it, when I was in a month ago, Josh said that his brother, Ham . . . he's a banker up Denver way, might know of some possible investors. He said it more like he was thinking out loud. But like I say, I ain't looking to sell my land. And if I got to, I'd rather sell to neighbors than some sucker back east."

"Let me explain how it would work. Let's suppose you did set up a corporation. I don't know what the figures would be, but let's say you had this corporation and issued four hundred thousand shares of stock at one dollar per share. You might transfer all your land and cattle, together with the debt on it, to the corporation for three hundred thousand shares of its stock."

"I don't see how that helps me none. What about the other hundred thousand shares?"

"You sell that to the investors at one dollar per share. The purchase price is paid to the corporation, but that leaves the corporation with one hundred thousand dollars in the bank."

The lean rancher pulled a handkerchief from his hip pocket and mopped at the beads of sweat that had erupted like fresh morning dew on his furrowed brow. "I'll be goddamned. It all sounds a might far-fetched, but that kind of cash would stock the ranch, pay off the open debt, and leave a couple of years operating money."

"Yes, and the beauty of it, Mr. Pierce, is that you don't pay anything for that money. You deliver the stock and if there is a profit, you might pay dividends. If not, you pay nothing."

"Then why in the hell would anybody pay hard cash for the stock?"

"Like I said earlier, they're gambling that it will become worth more as the underlying assets of land and cattle increase in value. And they're betting there will be future profits for dividends."

"But they'd still own a part of my ranch."

"Yes, but in the example I used, you would own seventy-five per cent of the shares. In a corporation, each share receives one vote. That means you have seventy-five per cent of the votes. You would elect the board of directors who, in turn, would elect you president. You would have total control, subject only to the responsibility to account to the shareholders for what's happening to the profits. In good years, you would decide how much money should be paid out as dividends and how much should be reinvested in the ranch."

"I don't see how any man could buy something he couldn't control. The way you put it, it sounds like I'm having my cake and eating it, too."

"I wouldn't know how to say it any better, Mr. Pierce. Oh, you'll have some bookkeeping headaches, and you may be troubled from time to time by a sense of responsibility to the other shareholders, but it would enable you to not only keep your ranching unit intact, but it might give you breathing room for future expansion."

His eyes lit up at that suggestion. It was not greed she saw there. She did not know what it was, but she had never met a rancher who did not covet his neighbor's land.

"I'll be damned if you don't about got me hog-tied into this corporation notion. But do you suppose you could get ahold of Ham Rivers and see if he can round up some investors? I'll stay in Santa Fe and cogitate on this a few days. Before I head back up to Taos, I'll stop by and let you know either way." A sheepish grin spread across his face. "You know, when I walked in here, I never dreamt I'd be asking you this—" He hesitated.

"What's that, Mr. Pierce?"

"Well, if I decided to get into this corporation business, I was wondering if you would handle the law wrangling part of it for me, and maybe be one of the board of directors you was talking about."

Danna smiled back. "I certainly would help you along with it as far as I can, but I don't know how long I'll be in Santa Fe."

Enoch Pierce rose to leave. "If Mr. Rivers has got the horse sense I think he's got, he'll see that you stay around and take care of my lawyering."

22

THE TENSE VOICES and the sound of running footsteps in the encampment jolted Josh awake. Reflexively, he sprang up and reached for his boots. No sooner had he pulled them on than She Who Speaks scrambled through the entryway of the tipi.

"What is it?"

"Soldiers. Bad Hand Mackenzie leads them. They are fighting up the canyon but will soon be here. Quickly. You must follow me."

Weaponless, Josh didn't have any better ideas, although it crossed his mind that Comanche, when attacked, often kill their prisoners.

Following the young woman, he bolted out of the tipi to be greeted by the acrid smell of gun smoke and burning hides. In the dusky, predawn light, he could see little but the shadowy forms of women and children dashing helter-skelter through the village, gathering up babies and what belongings they could hold in their arms, before abandoning the tipis and racing down the canyon, away from the increasing din of gunfire that inched nearer by the moment.

"This way."

Josh turned and chased after She Who Speaks, whose sleek body moved with the speed and grace of an antelope as she weaved through the maze of tipis. Finally, they broke into the clearing that separated the village from the western craggy canyon wall. His chest heaved and burned with pain as he trailed her across the lush grass. Knowing that his own body was tough and conditioned in comparison to those of most whites, he marveled at her stamina and endurance.

When they reached the shelter of some scattered boulders at the foot of the canyon wall, she signaled him to stop. When he caught up, he saw that another buck-skinned figure waited in the rocks. He was surprised when the lithe form with braided hair turned to face him. It was Jessica Chandler, stunning as ever, garbed in a deerskin shirt, calf-high moccasins, and only a narrow breechclout covering her perfect loins.

She smiled warmly, seemingly undaunted by whatever had happened during her captivity. "I knew it," Jessica said. "I knew they were bringing you here." She flew into his arms and hugged him enthusiastically before planting a moist kiss on his lips.

"Damn, I think I'll leave and come back again." He had all but forgotten She Who Speaks when the woman spoke with a sharp edge in her voice.

"You risk all of our lives with your childish games. I must lead you to your horses."

She raced away, darting past boulders and over the rocks scattered along the fringe of the canyon floor, until she led them to a crevice that split the red rock wall like a hatchet slash. Just inside, tethered to a jagged rock, were Josh's buckskin gelding and a coyote dun mare, both saddled with the recently developed double-cinched Texas rigs. Josh tried not to think what the Comanche might have done before stealing such saddles, which they would have taken only for future trade or sale, since their superior horsemanship necessitated only light, cradle-like saddles for their ponies.

"You will stay with the canyon wall," She Who Speaks said. "When it turns away from the morning sun, you will find a trail that will take you out. It is steep, but wider than the one that brought you in." She pointed to a small pile of gear and supplies that included several parfleche bags and paunches of water, as well as Josh's canteens. "You will find your weapons on the horses and food supplies for three, perhaps four, days. Many of the People will not know who you are, so you may have to protect yourselves. Your woman could be taken for Comanche if you are fortunate. Most of the warriors are defending the far end of the canyon, while the women and children escape. That will be to your benefit."

"Where is your horse?" Josh asked.

"I have no need for a horse. The Kwahadi have a hiding place one day and a night down the canyon. My husband's mother is on her way there now with my son. I will join them as soon as you leave."

"Then we'd better not waste any of your time." Josh began to sort through the supplies and tie them on his horse's saddle as Jessica followed his example. "You haven't told me about Erin McKenna . . . where do we meet her?"

"Eighteen sunrises, at the place where Buffalo Creek joins the Red River. You will bring the gold, and the trade will be made if you are not followed by soldiers."

"But I thought the McKenna girl would be allowed to return with us now."

"No. Quanah says only when the gold is delivered."

The wily war chief was still playing his cards cautiously. After the trail of broken promises left by the whites, Josh could not blame him, but he needed the McKenna girl now or some proof she was still alive.

"I must be able to satisfy the Court that she is alive, or I may not be able to arrange for the gold."

Jessica intervened. "I saw her, Josh. I spoke with her. Is that proof enough?"

"Damned if it shouldn't be. It looks like I've got my witness. Let's ride."

He helped Jessica onto her horse, and then, as he slid into his own saddle, he looked down at She Who Speaks, whose eyes met his with a look that was strangely sad. He found himself suddenly reluctant to leave. "Take care," Josh said. "I'll see you at the Red River."

"Ride with the wind, white warrior," she replied softly before she whirled and disappeared like some fading spirit behind the rocks.

"You have a way with women, white warrior," Jessica mocked, her voice teasing rather than cutting.

"Women have a way with me." He kicked the gelding's ribs gently and headed down the canyon, moving as much as possible under the shadowy cover of its overhanging rim. As the horses picked their way over the rugged terrain, Josh grew increasingly edgy. He had encountered no trouble with the fleeing Indians, but from the sound of gunfire and clanging sabers, the angry war cries and screams of pain, he knew that the battleground behind them was shrinking and that soon they could be in the middle of a bloody melee.

Jessica, in her Comanche attire, was likely a target for Army guns. His obvious whiteness would attract the Indians' wrath. Even if they were taken into custody by the Army, his mission might be fatally jeopardized. How would he explain his presence here? His chances of representing the Kwahadi in their pursuit for peace would be threatened as well.

No, for the moment, he and Jessica Chandler had no friends. They had to elude both Indians and whites.

Abruptly, the canyon wall veered left, and the fiery orange sun appeared over the eastern canyon rim and shot a beam of light that seemed to have been aimed to mark the trail. They reined in their horses for a moment while Josh surveyed their snakelike course. It was fortunate for the Indians that cavalry scouts had not located the trail, for the riders could move two abreast over most of it, and an assault funneled from both trails could have effectively closed off any retreat if the Army force were sufficiently large to contain the Indians. On the other hand, it would be easy for the soldiers to entrap themselves in this place. It was a daring, risky maneuver any way you looked at it.

The trail worried Josh, but he knew they had no choice. Many of the Comanche and Kiowa were making their exodus here, too. As near as he could tell, they were mostly women and children, but he knew that cornered, a Comanche woman could be as dangerous and deadly as a prairie badger. And the children were adept at killing at an early age.

Josh's fears proved unfounded. Indian women and children and several warriors passed them on their slow, steady climb up the steep trail. More than once they dismounted when the trail narrowed to have fleeing Comanche brush past them, seemingly oblivious to their presence there. The Indians probably assumed he was a Comanchero, Josh guessed, and a white woman in buckskins would not have attracted undue attention in Comanche or Kiowa encampments. He was reminded that most wild creatures don't attack unless their territory is infringed upon. He and Jessica gave the Indians all the room they wanted.

It was not until they had finally led their horses over the canyon rim, mounted, and headed at breakneck speed across the vast plains that spread before them to the west, that they ran into trouble. Three riders appeared, seemingly from nowhere, some distance behind Josh and Jessica and to their right. The riders bore down on them recklessly and relentlessly as they raced across the plains, and Josh knew that it didn't matter who the pursuers were, they would give no quarter. There wouldn't be any time for explaining.

At first, he thought they might be able to outrun the riders, but Jessica was an inexperienced rider and unable to push her mare to keep pace with Josh's buckskin. As the gap narrowed, he realized their flight was hopeless. "Keep riding," he yelled. "I'll catch up."

As Jessica's mare pulled away, he reined in the gelding, spun the horse around, yanking his Winchester from the saddle holster and leaping from the horse even before it had stopped. As the riders charged, he saw they were, as he had assumed, Indians. But unlike any Comanche he had seen, they were comparatively clumsy on their horses, exposing their bodies to rifle fire like no Comanche would have ever permitted. He aimed at the lead rider and squeezed the trigger. The rifle cracked and in nearly the same instant, the bare-chested Indian clutched his bullet-punctured body and toppled from his horse, falling beneath the pounding, slashing hooves of his comrades' mounts.

Josh could not fault their courage, for the survivors did not hesitate, but rode on. He fired again, but missed as the riders suddenly and wisely split and veered at angles from different directions, forcing him to shift attention from one in order to fire at the other. He swung his rifle to the left, pulled the trigger again, but got no response. Jammed. He flung down the rifle and drew his Navy revolver just as a dizzying blow caught him in the ribs and almost knocked him over. He shook off the searing pain and dropped to his knees, leveling his pistol at one squat Indian who had jumped from his horse and charged Josh, now with war axe raised. The Indian was close enough to splatter blood and shards of bone on Josh's own face when the bullet smashed into his jaw.

Josh rose on unsteady feet and turned to face the remaining attacker. When the thickly built Indian with his fiercely painted face lunged from his horse, he came down upon Josh with his bone-handled knife, slashing viciously. They fell to the rocky ground, and instinctively, Josh grasped the wrist of the Indian's knife hand. In the same instant, the Indian latched onto the wrist of his own gun hand. They rolled in the dust, locked like two bull elk engaged in a struggle in which only one would walk away.

Josh strained against the Indian's sinewy arm, dodging just in time as he relaxed his grip momentarily and the knife drove for the exact spot where his throat had been. Still, he held on desperately, tenaciously, like the jaws of a steel trap, only vaguely aware of the gnawing pain in his side, but knowing from the growing numbness that crept down his legs that he would never be a match for the quickness of his enemy if he ever let loose. Time and again, they changed places—first Josh on top, and then the Indian, as each fought to gain advantage, achieve the narrow edge that would make the difference between life and death. Josh sensed that time was on the Indian's side, for he could feel the growing fatigue and weakness that was consuming his body. It was as if a thousand leeches were sucking his strength away.

Suddenly, the Indian was on top again, throwing his full weight against the wrist of Josh's gun hand, slamming it against a protruding rock and knocking the pistol free from Josh's grip. Josh drove his knee savagely into the Indian's groin, and the crunching blow brought a moan of agony from its recipient. As the Indian wheezed and gasped frantically for breath, Josh twisted his wrist free from the attacker's grip. With a last burst of strength, he wrapped his newly freed arm over the Indian's neck, locking it in the crook of his elbow, closing it about the man's neck like a noose drawn tight, squeezing steadily, relentlessly, knowing that to weaken now was to die.

He could feel the Indian struggling to free his knife hand from Josh's iron grip on his wrist. He felt, too, the angry raking of his adversary's fingernails, like bear claws, at his eyes and face as they dug with desperation into his flesh. He could smell the warrior's sour breath, see the frantic bulging eyes and the contorted purple face that was only inches from his own, and finally he sensed strength ebbing from the Indian's body and then the utter limpness of it. Even then, he held on in spite of the swimming of his head and the fog glazing his eyes, until he was swallowed up by a dark abyss.

His next awareness was of something wet crawling over his face. He was half surprised when struck by the realization he was alive. His eyelids opened and he caught a glimpse of a hazy figure leaning over him before they closed again in reaction to the blinding rays of the Texas sun.

"Josh, can you hear me?"

A woman's voice. Jessica. He was alive . . . or in Heaven. Either way, it was better than what he'd expected. He shifted and opened his eyes again. "Yes, I hear you. I can't remember when I last heard such a pretty voice, like a babbling brook in the middle of a windswept desert."

"Save your charm, Mr. Rivers," she said with feigned sarcasm. "I think you had best concentrate your efforts on finding out if you can ride a horse in your condition."

"What condition?" He started to sit up but fell back down when the fire-like pain cut through the right side of his torso. "Damn!" he said, acutely aware now of the throbbing in his side.

Jessica sponged over his face with a damp rag she had torn from his shirt, and cradling his head with a gentle hand, she elevated his head slightly and pressed a canteen to his lips. "Drink first," she commanded.

He obeyed, washing the fuzziness out of his head with the lukewarm water that brought life to his parched, crusty throat and lips.

"There was an arrow imbedded between your ribs, all but a few inches of the shaft had been broken off."

"An arrow?" Josh said as he pushed away the canteen. "I didn't even know it. I remember being hit with something. The shaft must have snapped off during the struggle." He craned his neck, trying to get a look at his side, realizing only then that Jessica had made crude compresses from his shirt and had tied them around his chest with strips of leather she must have scavenged from the dead Indians.

"You took it out?"

"Yes, it wasn't in far. Must have glanced off your ribs and worked its way in between. Part of the arrowhead was still showing. You didn't seem wounded badly, but you had lost so much blood . . . I didn't know."

"I'll be alright, thanks to you. Do you think you can help me up now?"

"Are you sure?"

"No. But I don't see that we've got much choice."

She helped him up, and this time, he rose cautiously, tentatively, testing the limits of his mobility. When he was on his feet, he stretched his neck and arms, working the stiffness out of his legs while Jessica watched with a pleased smile on her face. Evidently satisfied that he could maintain his balance, Jessica eased away. Josh ran his fingers over the burning ridges that crisscrossed his nose and face. "Does it look as bad as it feels?"

"I don't know how it feels, but I'd guess it looks worse. Like somebody pushed your head in a sack with a mad tomcat."

"Thanks," he said sardonically.

"Oh, that's all right. I'm not all that interested in your face anyway," she said teasingly.

He shook his head in disbelief. The crazy woman. She just didn't appreciate what kind of danger they were in. Or didn't care. Or thrived on it.

Jessica walked just a short distance away to retrieve their horses. "I thought you were dead when I rode up. You were lying there, so still, both of you. But when I got close, I could see you were bleeding, and I pulled you out from under him. I would never have thought I would have had a chance of getting you on your feet in a matter of a few hours' time." She casually sidestepped the Indian he had shot with his revolver and soon returned leading the horses.

"You were supposed to keep riding," Josh said.

"Would you rather I had?"

"No."

"It's not that I'm that noble or heroic. I rode like the devil himself was chasing me for a spell, but then it suddenly occurred to me that I had not the slightest idea where I was or where I was going. Without you, these Indians or some others were bound to find me anyway. If they didn't, it was only a matter of time before I got lost and ran out of water and dried up out there on the plains someplace. I decided it was more practical for me to come back here and see if I could help in some way."

"Well, I'm damn glad you did, but you're lucky you didn't end up as somebody's dinner."

"Dinner?"

"These Indians . . . I just figured it out. I knew they weren't Comanche or Kiowa. They're Tonks."

"Tonks?"

"Tonkawa. People eaters . . . cannibals. Other tribes hate the Tonks because they eat their own kind. They consider human flesh a delicacy. They think they get courage from the flesh of a brave enemy. According to their way of thinking, it's a great honor to be eaten by a Tonk."

Jessica's face turned grim. For once, she had nothing to say.

"They scout for the soldiers," Josh said. "The Tonks and Comanche are ancestral enemies. They've been killing and mutilating each other for generations. The Tonks have something of an alliance with the whites; it gives them a chance to take revenge on their old enemies and get paid for it at the same time."

Jessica changed the subject. "Are you sure you can ride?"

"I'll have to."

23

JOSH LAY ON one of the saddle blankets in the den-like conclave of the brush-shrouded shelter. The crude lodge had the appearance of an upside-down bird's nest and was well hidden in the dense growth of cottonwood and tangle of gooseberry bushes and brush that surrounded it. They had put it together quickly, first clearing away a grassy spot and then piling on tree branches and loose brush, leaving just enough space in the center for them to barely sit up. They had to crawl on their hands and knees to get to their concealed sleeping quarters but so would any uninvited guests.

They had staked out the horses several hundred yards further down the arroyo. The animals were too spent to outrun any Indian visitors, and they decided that tying the horses nearby would be more likely to give away their hiding place.

It had been sheer luck, Josh thought, that they found this place. Of course, he had to give the buckskin's keen nose some of the credit. Mid-afternoon, when Josh had been on the verge of dropping, and when they had slowed their horses to a turtle's pace so that Jessica could help support him in the saddle, the buckskin had suddenly whinnied and picked up the deer trail and angled north of their westerly course. Josh had given his gelding the lead, thinking vaguely at the moment about the old adage "horse sense." It had been a good gamble. The buckskin had led them to a broad, shallow canyon, dense with trees and brush along the foot of its slopes. The creek bed, lush with fine-bladed buffalo grass, first appeared to be dry, but upon close examination it was found to be threaded by a shining narrow band of spring water that spilled over from natural limestone basins just below an outcropping of sandstone that seemed to emit tears through its porous surface.

If Josh had been in condition to go further, they would have ridden on after resting and watering the horses, for the presence of water and grass in the arroyo also made it a likely stopping place for Comanche or other travelers of the plains. But they had decided to risk it and perhaps stay over another day, concluding that a strengthened Josh would improve their chances in the long run. Besides, Josh had noted that none of the Indians escaping the attacking soldiers had seemed headed in this direction. Life was a series of risks; their holing up in the small, box-canyon would just have to be another.

Dusk was surrendering to shadowy darkness now, and Josh began to worry a bit about Jessica's whereabouts. After they had built their shelter, they bathed at the springs. Jessica had peeled off her scanty Indian garb and began to scrub away the red dust that coated her skin as if unaware that Josh was present.

He had not been unaware of her. It had been impossible for him not to watch her: firm breasts that seemed molded to her even when she bent to wash her feet and ankles and the wet, sable hair gleaming like an otter's fur in the iridescent sun. He noted the gentle rounded slopes of her buttocks and the thick, lush foliage that sensuously shrouded her parted thighs.

Her eyes met his only once, and the suggestion he saw there was enough to start the smoldering of his too-long dormant loins. But she had turned her head and moved away to slip back into her buckskin shirt and scanty breechclout and pull her moccasins up to cover the smooth white flesh that ended where her crimson, sunburned skin began. Then, in subdued silence, she cleaned his wound and bound it again.

After returning from the spring, they had gluttonized the parfleche of pemmican, after which Josh had stretched out on the saddle blanket they had spread out in the shelter and instantly dropped into a deep sleep. Now, he guessed he had been asleep for the better part of four hours. He took a drink from his canteen; the sleep had been good medicine. He still felt weak, but the soreness from his ribs was not intolerable if he was careful and deliberate in his movements.

Suddenly, he tensed and reached for his revolver. Someone was outside the shelter—someone who had moved in close without his hearing. Through the cracks between the piled brush and branches, he could make out a moving form. But it was too dark to tell much else. It could be Jessica, but then again, it might not be.

The shadowy figure swooped down, and he could hear the crackling of brush and the scrape of leather against grass as a body wormed through the burrow-like entryway toward Josh. Still he did not speak, leveling his pistol at the entryway. Suddenly, Jessica's smiling face appeared, and he breathed a sigh of relief and lowered the pistol.

"You scared the hell out of me," he said as she slipped in beside him. "I thought you were an Indian. Why didn't you say something?"

"I thought maybe you were still asleep. I didn't want to wake you."

"You came in so quietly."

"I was trying to. I watched the Comanche children play in the village. I thought it was fascinating the way they sneaked up on each other without making a sound. It could be a good thing to learn in this country, don't you agree?"

"I won't argue with that. Where have you been?"

"I went to check the horses. Then I just walked. It won't be easy living in a city again, after having all of these miles and miles of open space."

"Yeah, with Comanche breathing down your neck every minute."

"I don't have that much trouble understanding the Comanche. There is something romantic about their way of life. It's so simple, so free."

"There's nothing romantic about having your brains beat out with a war axe."

"Josh, you know what I'm talking about. Their way of life—“

"Yes, it has its attractions. And if you were raised with it, it would be hard to imagine living any other way, but I find your reaction to all of this rather strange."

"You do? Why?"

"Well, I know you've had rough times in your life, not the least of which has been this past week. But you've been in all of the biggest cities of this country, enjoyed all of the conveniences civilization has to offer, basked in the worship of cheering audiences. Now here we are, out in the middle of what some people would call Hell, and I could swear you're actually enjoying yourself."

She took his hand and squeezed it. "But I am. I love these plains. The vastness of it. Sometimes I feel like I just want to take off running, drink it all in, run until I drop. Oh, I love being an actress, too, and I find the cities exciting. I guess I just live for the now. And the now is here. The now is you and me." Her natural enthusiasm was contagious, for that was all he could think about for the moment. The now. Her and him.

She edged closer to him, placed her hand gently upon his bare chest and began gently raking and curling the wiry hair there. Her fingers trudged a path down his belly and then backtracked and brushed his nipples, teasingly, setting his hunger for her nearly out of control. As if reading his thoughts, she said, her voice strangely husky, "You have to be careful . . . your wound. Lie back. I'll make love to you this time."

He was unresisting, and as he cautiously let himself back down on the blanket, Jessica removed his trousers and checked to see if there was life beneath them. Apparently convinced, he heard the chafing of buckskin against flesh as she wriggled out of her own garments. Then he felt her easing over him, straddling his hips, almost weightless, sliding herself gently back and forth with a steady, agonizingly slow rhythm. She purred, and he could feel her begin to constrict. She moaned and finally gasped and shuddered as he drained his seed.

Later, as she lay drowsily beside him, curled up with the soft flesh of her bottom molded to his thigh, and her head nestled in his arm, it occurred to Josh, guiltily, that in the frenzy of escape, survival, and lust, he had nearly forgotten the purpose of his mission.

"Jessica," he said softly. "Are you still awake?"

"Barely," she replied with a sleepy voice.

"The McKenna girl. You're sure it was her that you saw."

"That's who she said she was. Flaming red hair, green eyes. I suppose men would call her beautiful. The Comanche didn't mind that we talked. We were left alone for an hour or better. They probably wanted me to hear what she had to say."

"What do you mean?"

"She's not all that unhappy with the Comanche. In fact, she's not sure she wants to return to her people. She loves her father's ranch, but with him gone, she feels there is nothing to go back to. She's the fourth wife of a warrior whose family has some stature in the village. She hasn't been cruelly treated, and while she does not love her husband, she does not hate him, and she's grown very fond of his first wife. She accepts her fate, whatever it is. She feels she had no choice in the matter anyway."

"Doesn't she miss her aunt?"

"Oh, yes. She seems to care very much for her aunt, but she is afraid that if she goes back, she will just cause more grief for both of them."

"Why should that be?"

"Her belly is swollen like a ripe melon. She'll bear her husband's child within a few months." Jessica's voice had trailed off, and soon the even rise and fall of her chest told Josh she was asleep, leaving him to listen alone to the mournful howling of coyotes in the distance. He heard the eerie hooting of an owl in the cottonwood outside their lair, as he pondered the future of the young woman whose presumed happiness he was supposed to rescue out here on the Llano Estacado.

24

STANDING AT FIVE feet ten inches without her shoes, Danna Sinclair was an exceedingly tall woman by the standards of her era, but she did not think of herself as being tall. The young woman with alert cocoa brown eyes who approached her as she stepped from the Rivers Law Office with folders tucked securely under her arms was at least five inches shorter than Danna, but Danna judged her as tall. Perhaps it was the quiet, confident way in which she carried herself, or the way her chestnut-colored hair swept back over her head and shoulders like waves on a turbulent sea, or the willow-like quality of her frame. There was something vaguely familiar about the woman, but Danna could not place her.

Then it struck her. This would be Tabitha Rivers.

Danna stepped toward Josh's sister, extending her hand and smiling warmly. "You're Tabitha Rivers? I'm so pleased to meet you."

Tabitha crinkled her nose, her smile bright against smooth olive-tinted skin, as she accepted Danna's hand. "I'm Danna Sinclair."

"How did you know who I was?"

"I can't say. Your eyes, perhaps. They're Josh's and Cal's. Somehow you have Rivers written all over you, Tabitha."

"Please call me Tabby. I'm sorry I didn't stop to meet you earlier. The *New Mexican* sent me up to Taos to cover a story. I just got back yesterday. Cal's told me all about you. And this McKenna case you're involved in."

"I'm on my way to the federal building now," Danna said. "The case is set for hearing before Judge Robinson this morning, but I haven't heard anything from Josh. I'm going to present a motion for continuance, but from what I've heard, Judge Robinson will not be predisposed to take it kindly."

The two women moved back under the shade of the portals to evade the baking heat of the morning sun. "Judge Robinson," Tabby spat contemptuously, "empties Oliver McKenna's chamber pot, drinks its contents, and even likes it if he is told to do so. He's pig shit."

Tabitha Rivers had a way with words, and she certainly didn't mince them.

"Well, all I can do is try. Strange things happen in the courtroom. Maybe I'll find a way yet to put him in a corner, so he has to give me more time."

"If you don't mind, I'd like to go with you," Tabby said. "My presence might not hurt. Judge Robinson knows that I'm a reporter for *The Santa Fe New Mexican*. In spite of his deference to his lordship, Sir Oliver, the good judge is very thin skinned about public opinion. He aspires to higher callings. Perhaps a territorial governorship. And he won't overtly abuse his discretion in front of the press."

"For my part," Danna said, "you'll be welcome at the hearing, although I can't honestly say that the judge's ruling against me at this point would be considered an overt abuse of discretion."

The two women crossed the plaza and walked briskly along the shaded adobe walls of the Palace of the Governors toward the federal building. "I wonder what happened to Cal?" Danna said. "He had planned to meet me this morning. He was concerned that McKenna would put his assassins to work again."

"Don't look behind you, but Cal is following us about twenty paces back. He trusts very few, that brother of mine, and he's always got his eye out for trouble. Too many months scouting, I guess. Actually, I can't imagine McKenna using his hired guns in Santa Fe, or if he did, he'd be very discreet about it. He has political influence here, of course, but he doesn't own the city. There are other powerful men here looking for an excuse to tie Oliver McKenna to some illegal shenanigans."

"Besides," Danna observed, "there's no cause to have me shot if they can take me down in the courtroom and remain perfectly respectable and law abiding in the course of it."

25

THE ONLY COLOR in the courtroom where Judge Andrew Robinson presided was the American flag draped from the wall behind the judge's bench. The remainder of the cramped room was furnished and decorated in one hue of brown or another. Plastered adobe walls painted dirty beige; ceiling beams, stained walnut; solid functional railings and chairs and counsel tables, another variation of brown. Courtrooms were drab places, Danna thought, as she sat alone at the defense table some fifteen minutes before the ten o'clock hearing, her eyes scanning the courtroom so she would be familiar and comfortable with the surroundings before the hearing commenced. She straightened the bodice of her cotton dress and noted that the fabric was an olive brown color, another contributor to the room's drabness.

She always made it a practice to be in the courtroom early; she was impatient with tardiness in others and did not tolerate it in herself. But she also used her habit of early arrival as a tool to help her scrutinize and appraise the participants, judge the emotional state of the witnesses and ferret out some clue to her opponents' strategies.

There were no more than a dozen spectators in two short rows behind the railing that separated them from the traditional arena; overcrowding would not be a problem. There would not be more than a few people in Santa Fe who had heard of the obscure case bearing the impressive title, "In the matter of the Estate of William McKenna." It was a typical case, important only to those directly involved.

Cal and Tabby Rivers, sitting in chairs only a few feet behind Danna, were the only other persons in the room. They sat quietly, respecting her need for thinking time.

Danna turned when the door at the rear of the courtroom creaked open. Three men walked in. The first two moved briskly and business-like down the narrow aisle and took their places at the other counsel table. The third peeled away and took a seat in the spectators' section directly behind his companions. Danna did not recognize the third man, but he obviously led a different life than the other two. His age could have been anywhere between forty and sixty, for his skin was dark and dry and cracked like parched earth from years in the sun. His shaggy shoulder-length hair was black with the exception of long strands of white that striped the middle of his scalp like the hair on a skunk's back. He stretched his neck back and forth and tugged uneasily at the gray coat that hung loosely on his wiry frame. Whoever he was, he likely had not donned a suit in twenty years, Danna guessed. He was a man of the outdoors with strains of Indian or Mexican blood doubtless running in his blood. The other two men, who had not even acknowledged her presence, were huddled at their table. They were so different, yet so much alike.

The top of Oliver McKenna's head was as shiny as polished marble, his jowly face shaved smooth, and vested belly protruding as though with child. His lawyer, Peter Dimona, had a full head of distinguished iron-gray hair and a complementing pencil-thin mustache. His flesh was spare on a slight, almost effeminate, frame that stretched to about five and a half feet.

Yet they were only different shapes cut from the same cloth. They were stylishly dressed men who looked like they had never been touched by the burning sun or moisture-sucking air of the great Southwest, both acutely caught up in their own self-importance. Most men sought money, even power, in one form or another. These were two men who already had money and power, yet lusted for more with a hunger that was insatiable.

Again the door behind her opened, and a white-haired Mexican man walked in the room and announced with a thick accent, "The Circuit Court of the District of New Mexico is now in Session, Judge Andrew Robinson presiding. All rise."

Danna had never appeared in Judge Robinson's court and was surprised when a tall, trim man with salt and pepper hair strode through the door and made his way to the elevated judge's bench. Danna judged him to be in his early forties, some twenty years younger than she expected. It occurred to her that she had not done her homework on the judge. She knew him by reputation and public philosophy, but sometimes that counted for less than the personal characteristics.

"Be seated," the judge said as he took his own chair and commenced shuffling through the sheets of papers on his bench. After several moments, he looked up, fixing his eyes first on Danna.

She had the feeling that his pale blue eyes were seeing her in a different kind of bar than that of his court. She was not always offended when she observed a man undressing her mentally, but she was in this case. Nonetheless, she met his gaze firmly, but not belligerently, for her client's fate was in this man's hands.

"This case is before the court," the Judge said, his gaze still set on Danna, "on the Petition of Mr. Oliver McKenna, for final determination of the heirs at law of William McKenna." The judge had a resonant voice, Danna noted. The words rolled off his tongue like warm maple syrup. A politician's voice. She suspected that most women found him appealing, but of course they could not vote.

The judge shifted in his chair and turned to Peter Dimona. "Counselor, the court is considering your petition. Are you ready to proceed with the evidence?"

Danna rose from her chair. "May it please the court."

With a look of mild exasperation, the judge turned his attention back to Danna. "Yes, Miss Sinclair, I believe? It escapes me for the moment. What is your interest in this proceeding?"

"I represent Miss Dawn Rutledge. Erin McKenna's aunt. Erin is the daughter of the late William McKenna and as such, his sole heir."

The judge looked down at the papers in front of him. "I believe the petition alleges that Oliver McKenna is the sole heir. I am afraid you will have to clarify yourself, Miss Sinclair."

Danna had the feeling the Judge was baiting her. Although Judge Robinson's predecessor had handled prior hearings, it was highly unlikely the judge had entered the hearing cold. More likely, he had been well briefed, possibly by Dimona, and he certainly would have reviewed the court file.

"I believe you will find, Your Honor, that prior to Oliver McKenna's appointment as administrator, I filed an objection on Miss Rutledge's behalf to his appointment on the grounds of conflict of interest. If you will—"

"One moment, please, Miss Sinclair. You stated you are representing Miss Rutledge. I fail to see that Miss Rutledge has any interest at all, and it would therefore follow that you have no standing before the court."

"Your Honor, I believe the court records will show that over the objection of Mr. McKenna, Dawn Rutledge was appointed Guardian ad litem to act on Erin McKenna's behalf in her absence. Judge Davis entered the order the same day Oliver McKenna was appointed administrator."

The judge's lips pinched together, and Danna could see that he was vexed. He was doubtless searching his mind for some excuse to invalidate Dawn Rutledge's appointment and thereby proceed to consider Dimona's uncontested evidence. Perhaps she could give him cause to act more prudently.

"Your Honor, at this time, I would ask the court to enter the name of my co-counsel in your notes."

The judge sighed. "I should think it would be more appropriate for your co-counsel to speak for himself. Or is it herself?" he added sarcastically.

"My co-counsel is Mr. Joshua Rivers. He cannot be present today, Your Honor, because he is traveling in the Indian Territory, retrieving evidence that is critical to this case."

A slight lifting of the judge's dark eyebrows gave away his curiosity.

Danna continued. "My co-counsel's brother and sister are present in the courtroom. You may have heard of Calvin Rivers who has scouted for Mackenzie's Fourth Cavalry. And of course, Tabitha Rivers, who writes for *The Santa Fe New Mexican*. She thought her newspaper might find this case worthy of reporting."

The judge shot a meaningful glance at Dimona, whose seemingly fleshless face might have been chiseled from ice it was so emotionless. Suddenly wary, he straightened in his chair and spoke, his voice laced with sarcasm. "Miss Sinclair, I have found our little dialogue interesting,but not very enlightening. You have yet to state why you rose to address this court. I hope it would not be imposing upon your sensibilities too greatly to ask you to do so at this time."

"I apologize, Your Honor, I have digressed. At this time, I would like to move the court for a one-month continuance of the hearing on Oliver McKenna's petition."

The judge glowered, and Peter Dimona leaped to his feet and was before the bench with the same single fluid motion an expert horseman might mount his horse. "Your Honor," Dimona said in a soft voice that had a rhythmic quality to it, "this motion for continuance is entirely out of order here. The date of this hearing has been known to all parties for more than six weeks. There is no reason that this young lady should appear here and say she is not ready to proceed."

Danna sloughed off Dimona's condescending reference to her. "Your Honor, my motion must be ruled upon before you proceed with any hearing on Oliver McKenna's petition. I am entitled to present an argument in support of my motion."

A look of exasperation crossed the judge's face. "Miss Sinclair, kindly refrain from telling me what the court must do." Then he spoke to the Mexican bailiff who stood near the doorway at the back of the room. "Señor Gomez, do you have a timepiece on your person?"

The old man dug into his trousers pocket and pulled out an enormous gold pocket watch. "*Si*, Your Honor," he replied, holding up the watch.

"Very well. You will keep time for us. Miss Sinclair will have twenty minutes and Mr. Dimona will have twenty minutes. If Miss Sinclair chooses, she may save part of her twenty minutes for rebuttal. Are there any objections? Mr. Dimona?"

"None, Your Honor."

"Miss Sinclair?"

"None, Your Honor, but I would like to reserve five minutes for rebuttal. So, if you will have the bailiff inform me when I have used up my first fifteen, I would be most grateful."

"Señor Gomez, you heard Miss Sinclair's request?"

"*Si*, Your Honor. I shall do so."

As Peter Dimona moved back to his chair, Danna saw the confident smile he gave the fidgety Oliver McKenna. "You can speak in support of your motion, Miss Sinclair," the judge said.

Danna moved from behind the counsel table and approached the judge's bench. "Your Honor, there is a single compelling reason why this court should grant a continuance of the hearing on Oliver McKenna's petition for determination of heirship. The reason? Simply that Erin McKenna is the sole heir to William McKenna's estate, and there is every reason to believe she is alive. But her presence in this courtroom is necessary to establish that fact. To make any decision without having exhausted every possibility of proving that Erin McKenna is alive has the potential of making the circuit court of this territory look like a prairie dog court."

Danna turned slightly away from the judge, looking significantly at Tabitha who signaled with a wink that she had picked up her cue and began to write hurriedly on the pad she held on her lap. Danna swung her attention back to the judge. "I say this with all due respect, Your Honor . . . your court is something like a bastard child. There aren't many out here quite ready to claim it. If it goes bad, they never will. But if it comes down solid for justice, it won't be long and it will be welcomed with open arms. So, in a sense, every time this court hears a case, it is on trial itself, and someday, the people will render their verdict." Danna could see that Judge Andrew Robinson was no longer mocking her, and he was not pleased with what he was hearing. His manner, the tautness of his jaw, told her he was ill at ease. But she had his undivided attention for the moment.

"Your Honor, I submit that nothing mandates an immediate decision on this case. William McKenna's estate is being administered now by the man who seeks to be judged his sole heir. If he is so certain of his position, can it matter that he be required to wait another few months to have a final determination made? Is there any real justification for the court to be stampeded into making a determination in favor of Oliver McKenna? I believe that Erin McKenna is alive, Your Honor. I freely acknowledge that I could be mistaken in this belief. But if I am not, and this court proceeds today to determine that Oliver McKenna is the sole heir of his brother's estate, what verdict will the people of this territory render upon this court when Erin McKenna rides into Santa Fe and asks why she was left, not only orphaned, but penniless? All I am asking for is time. I said earlier that Josh Rivers was in Indian Territory retrieving evidence. The evidence, Your Honor, is Erin McKenna."

In her remaining time, Danna hammered repeatedly at the point that justice would not be aborted by waiting. Just before her fifteen minutes expired, she said, "I would not for one moment impugn the integrity of this court, but we cannot ignore the fact that the petitioner in this case is a very prominent and influential man. Yes, a year has passed since William McKenna's death, but it is common knowledge that many estates take several years, or more, to settle. But the petitioner is unwilling to wait for another few months, even a single month, to foreclose the rights of Erin McKenna and claim the inheritance as his own. Yes, he has a legal right to force a decision upon the issue of heirship, but at this time in our history, we cannot disregard appearances."

Danna spun around and returned to her seat, leaving Judge Robinson to chew on the implications of her words.

Peter Dimona did not seem the least ruffled by Danna's argument. He bowed slightly to her as he rose and stepped forward with a benign smile frozen on his otherwise impassive face. Before he spoke, he formed a little tipi with the long slender fingers of his perfectly manicured hands. He gazed at them for several moments as if drawing divine inspiration from some invisible force floating through the space between his palms. Then he slowly lifted his head, and his face suddenly became grim, almost masked with sadness. "At first, Your Honor," he said, his voice so muted that Danna leaned forward to hear, "I excused the young lady for the cutting and uncharitable attacks she made upon the petitioner."

What attacks? Danna wondered. If they considered what she had said as "attacks," then they were going to see murder in her rebuttal.

"I am inclined to give considerable leeway to the gentler sex, and I made due allowances for Miss Sinclair's inexperience, but the court can surely appreciate that I cannot let her defamatory remarks go unanswered. By innuendo, if not by outright accusation, Miss Sinclair has contended that the petitioner has some devious motive in bringing the petition before the court."

He looked at Danna and shook his head in disbelief. "This is pure hogwash, and it is an insult to the circuit court for counsel to make such irresponsible statements. My client has been acting as administrator of his brother's estate for more than a year. Lawyers have been criticized by press and public for their delaying and dilatory ways . . . courts for their slow and cumbersome procedures. If we are truly concerned about respect for the law and our judicial system, then it appears that it would behoove us all to work toward the speedy and just conclusions of cases before the bar. Your Honor, by denying Miss Sinclair's motion for continuance, you are not prejudging the merits of our petition. If we do not satisfy our burden of proof and fail to produce sufficient evidence to establish that Oliver McKenna is the sole heir of his brother, and thereby entitled to distribution of his estate, the court may simply deny the petition. For your edification, I wish to inform you, however, that we have evidence that Erin McKenna is, in fact, dead. There is a witness in this courtroom, Mr. Buck Tripp, a frontiersman of some reputation, who has returned with skeletal remains identified by a Comanche warrior as those of Erin McKenna's. He also has a turquoise ring which the warrior stated he took from the poor girl's body. This ring can be positively identified as one given to Erin by her late father. We are asking only that you proceed in this matter, that you allow our evidence, consider it carefully, then make the ruling you consider appropriate. I have not used my allotted time, but anything else I might say would be redundant and a further imposition on the valuable time of this court. I do hope the young lady will reconsider her remarks and see fit to render a public apology to Oliver McKenna who is truly one of the distinguished citizens of this territory and has suffered quite enough already as the result of the tragic murders of his brother and niece."

Dimona's eyes bore into Judge Robinson's, locking them almost hypnotically. "Hear our evidence, Your Honor. Then decide. That is all that we ask. Deny Miss Sinclair's motion for a continuance."

As Peter Dimona walked confidently back to his chair, Danna had a sinking feeling in her stomach that the diminutive lawyer, who seemed to swoop and strike like a bird of prey and then steal away again, had mouthed precisely the right words. All Judge Robinson wanted was something to get his feet out of the fire. Dimona had done better than that: he had put the fire out.

Danna rose for her rebuttal but was so absorbed in organizing her thoughts, she did not realize until she was in front of the judge's bench that all eyes were fixed on the rear of the courtroom. She turned and saw why. There stood Josh Rivers, a sheepish grin on his face. With him was a buckskin-clad woman who looked every bit an Indian except for the white cast of her skin. Who was she? She was not Erin McKenna, for her hair was black, not red. And she was somewhat older than the McKenna girl. Whoever she was, she was devastatingly beautiful, extremely poised in spite of her primitive attire. And her smooth half-naked thighs had the attention of every man in the room.

"Your Honor," Danna said, "I request a five-minute recess."

26

"IF YOU HADN'T shown up when you did, it would have been the last roundup for us," Danna said, while Josh carved another healthy chunk of meat off the rare beef steak that nearly covered his plate and forked it into his mouth. His reply was a shrug. He had not yet had an opportunity to talk at length with Danna about the developments in the McKenna case. A hot bath and shave had come first. Then there was the need to make arrangements for Jessica.

Cal had insisted upon relieving him of that chore. Josh had no doubt that the two of them would hit it off just fine, likely end up sharing a bed in Jessica's room this night, or the next, at the latest. Josh felt no pangs of jealousy. Jessica was a special breed of woman: strong, independent, a born survivor—the kind of woman he could love, but didn't. There were no permanent commitments between them, but there would always be a bond. They would always be dear friends, but a future romantic relationship was far from certain.

He gave another thought to his brother. He had noticed an exchange of glances between Cal and Danna that hinted at some secret between them. Surely Cal had not romanced Danna. No. Impossible.

He continued to devour the steak in an efficient, business-like manner. He looked up and saw that Danna was watching him, her green eyes sparkling in the reflection of the lamplight. She was smiling at him in the benevolent way that a mother smiles at her child. At least she was not pressing him for the serious conversation he had promised when he suggested they meet in the dining room of the Exchange to discuss the events of the past weeks and to plot their next moves.

She had already eaten her steak and fried potatoes that accompanied it. Josh was working on his second steak and had downed a thick piece of fresh-baked apple pie in between.

Damn, she was something to look at tonight. Her burgundy gown scooped low enough to show just a tantalizing hint of cleavage between the smooth white swell of her breasts. Her face almost seemed framed by a glowing moon, so sleek and shiny was the long hair that fell over her shoulders.

He thought of the women who were important to him at this time of his life: Jessica; the hot-blooded Constanza; the elusive She Who Speaks. And of course, Danna. It was strange, he thought, how women could be so different, yet be equally beautiful and alluring in ways that defied comparison. He respected women, perhaps deluded himself that he had some understanding of them. But there was always an element of mystery hidden in every one of them. And Danna Sinclair was the biggest mystery to him of all.

He cleaned up the remnants of his supper and washed it down with black coffee. Women. They had a way of getting a hold on him like hard liquor did on other men.

"Eating may keep you from talking," Danna said, "but it certainly doesn't keep you from thinking. Your mind has been working like a cowboy's rope all the time we've been sitting here. It's been almost as busy as your stomach."

"I've been thinking about you."

The impish smile faded from her lips. "There are more pressing problems. We'd both better start thinking about the McKenna case . . . and your law practice, if you expect to hang onto it. Now tell me, how did you happen to know just when to show up this morning?"

"Just plain luck. Oliver McKenna looked like he'd just been kicked in the balls after Jessica finished testifying, didn't he?"

"Well, I'm not an expert on such things. But he did look like a very sick man, I must admit. Mr. Dimona seemed relatively unfazed, though. Whatever runs in his veins is ice cold. He's an excellent lawyer . . . as good as there is . . . if ethics don't count. The important thing is that we got the continuance. With Jessica's testimony that she had talked to Erin McKenna, and Tabby being in the courtroom to report it, Judge Robinson didn't have any choice. But thirty days . . . is that enough time?"

"It'll have to be. We're going to have to make some decisions."

Josh told Danna, who listened intently, about the agreements he had made with Quanah Parker's proxy and of his and Jessica's escape from the canyon which he had since learned was known as Palo Duro. "According to the news I've picked up here in Santa Fe," Josh said, "Quanah wasn't captured by Mackenzie at Palo Duro. The Fourth Cavalry doesn't think he was there. I know better. Erin McKenna was apparently there, too, but that doesn't mean she lived through it. We won't know that until the gold is delivered."

"But tell me, Josh, how do you know the Comanche can be trusted?"

"For one thing, they need me . . . us. Quanah knows his way of life is about over. He is a young man, not more than thirty. Mark my word, he's not going to dry up in a reservation out in the middle of nowhere. He's going to chop out a place for himself in the white man's world, but he needs somebody else to negotiate terms and do it discreetly, so both sides can save face. Beyond that, from what Cal told me and from everything I've heard, Quanah Parker's an honorable man. Some folks call him a murderer, but nobody's ever called him a liar."

"There's a problem, though. I assume you've considered it: the gold. Oliver McKenna controls the Circle M assets. I doubt if Dawn Rutledge has the money to fund the ransom."

"I've thought about it, alright, and I plan to find out just how deep into his poke Pop's willing to dig for his old friend, Bill McKenna."

"What do you mean?"

"I got into this as a favor to my old man."

"You got into it for money, too," Danna corrected.

He grinned sheepishly. "Yeah, that too. But if Pop wants to save Erin McKenna, he's going to have to stake her some money. I know he doesn't have the cash, but he doesn't have much debt, and he can probably borrow it. If he'll gamble that much, we can get her back. I'll stay around here for a few days, to see if I can help put things in order. Cal is going to ride up to the Slash R, and, assuming Pop backs us, they'll come back here and make arrangements for the gold. After that, Cal and I will head for the rendezvous with Quanah. Now, that's enough of McKenna. We can talk more about that tomorrow. There's something else I'd like to discuss with you."

"What's that?"

Josh signaled the waiter. "Juan, can we have a bottle of wine, please? A red wine would do fine."

"*Si*, señor."

Josh continued. "George Hatter was in my room late this afternoon."

"You, no doubt, learned how much your law clerk adores me," Danna said sarcastically.

"George doesn't know what to make of you. You annoy the hell out of him."

"Tell me something I don't know."

"I shall. George also respects you, thinks you're the best damned lawyer he's ever run into . . . that includes his present employer. His words, not mine."

"I can't quite believe what you're saying. Mr. Hatter's been very curt with me since my arrival, and I haven't found him very cooperative."

"Hell, he's curt with me, too, and uncooperative. He'll never pass the bar. He's a hell of a good law clerk, and that's what he'll be his whole life. He's also a very good office manager. George says that if you open up an office across the plaza, three-fourths of my clients will march right over there. He's smart enough to know that he prospers if my office prospers. He thinks I should hire you to work in our office. Interested?"

"Not very."

His eyes narrowed in disbelief. "I've seen your office in Madison. You have nothing to go back to there. There's no future in that little cow town. And the challenges Santa Fe has to offer . . . there's no comparison."

"But I'm my own boss in Madison. I don't know that I want to work for someone else, pick up someone else's garbage. You have a diversified practice, Josh. The opportunities are unlimited. I should think that over the next several years, a half dozen lawyers could be put to work in your office. Your reputation already extends beyond the boundaries of Santa Fe and into New Mexico territory. But you've got to keep the weeds cut on the home place, as the farmers say."

"That's why I want you to go to work for me. So that somebody can get a handle on the office practice."

"No, I'm very complimented that you asked me, but I just don't think it would work."

The waiter arrived with the bottle of wine and two goblets. He filled the glasses as Josh and Danna sat there, facing each other in the dusky room, oblivious to the chatter of the tables that surrounded them. Josh sipped at his wine and sat silently for some moments, toying with the wine glass. Danna's eyes were fixed on his, and he sensed that she was trying to read him as much as he was her. He suddenly realized she was playing poker with him. Her hand wasn't over; she was just waiting for him to deal his next card.

"What if I made you an associate, paid you a salary plus a percentage of the gross with an agreement that if things worked out you could become a partner in a few years?"

"Frankly, Josh, I don't find it very intriguing. I'm head of my own firm now. The only thing you're offering is a title. I'd still be working for you, and if you chose not to make me a partner a few years from now, I will have wasted those years of my life."

Her attitude was starting to irritate him. "You will have had a few years' experience that you wouldn't have got sitting on your fanny back in Madison."

"That's speculation on your part. And I'm not necessarily married to Madison. I could open an office in Santa Fe. You've already said that your law clerk thinks I might not starve here."

Damn, he had shown his cards too early. He finished his glass of wine and poured another. He noted that hers was still nearly full. There was no warmth in her face now; nor anger. He thought of Peter Dimona. Josh sighed. "A partnership. Eighty-twenty to start out. Fifty-fifty in five years."

"Who has the eighty?"

Was she serious? Was she just gouging him out of meanness with her spurs? "I'd have the eighty, of course. I established the office."

"Perhaps. But you're also pissing it away," she said, cuttingly. "I'm confident you aren't going to change your wandering ways, so I'd be staying in the office doing eighty percent of the work. I just assumed I'd be paid a commensurate share of the profits."

He gulped down the wine and poured another glass, knowing he was past his limit already. "Damn it, woman. There're a hundred lawyers who would jump at this opportunity. I don't know what else I could do."

"There's not another lawyer who would make a better partner for you, Josh." It was a matter of fact statement.

"Alright, this is my last offer. Fifty-fifty. But you have to buy a half interest in the library and office furniture. I'll take your note for it."

"How much interest on the note?"

He was incredulous. "How much interest? Oh, hell, none. And you can pay it off over five years. I'll sell everything at cost, less forty percent."

"And what will we call this firm?"

"Well, I hadn't thought about it. I didn't exactly come here tonight with the idea I was going to walk away with a law partner. I suppose Rivers and Sinclair."

"I think Sinclair and Rivers has a nicer ring. It rolls off the tongue better, don't you think? Just say it: Sinclair and Rivers."

Josh finished his third glass of wine, but fought off the temptation to pour a fourth. He remembered now why he usually avoided spirits: low tolerance. "No, damn it. You've pushed me far enough. It's Rivers and Sinclair, or you can forget about it."

She smiled mischievously, and he realized she had been teasing him, that he had lost his sense of humor two drinks back.

"Then you agree?"

"Tentatively. I'll draft a proposed partnership agreement tomorrow. If the terms are satisfactory to both of us, then we have a partnership. And there's one other thing that has to be understood."

"I'm listening."

"This is a business partnership, nothing more."

"However you want it," he snapped, wondering now if he had made a mistake he would regret.

As if reading his mind, Danna said, "Don't worry, you won't be sorry. I'll be a good partner and a good friend."

27

"DO YOU PLAN to stay here at the Exchange?" Josh asked as he stood with Danna in the lobby.

"No, I think not. Now that my immediate future is more or less settled, I'll be looking for something more permanent."

"I've been living here for three years now. It's close to the office and the plaza, and I wouldn't think there would be a safer place for an unmarried lady."

"I think I can see to my own safety. I've been doing that for a long time. What you say about the convenience is, of course, true, and the accommodations are very nice. But it is also very expensive. I don't think that living here would be very prudent management of my funds."

Josh thought he caught the hint of a mild rebuke in her voice.

"Your sister, Tabby, has advised me to look at an adobe *casita* just off the Trail Road east of the plaza. She's interested in buying it and thought we might be able to purchase it together. We could share expenses and split up the household chores. It seems she doesn't like washing dishes any better than I do."

"You were planning this all the whole time, weren't you? I've got a feeling I've been out-maneuvered."

She did not answer his question. "I'll see you at the office in the morning," she said, and moved toward the stairway that led to her second floor room. "We can review some of the cases that need immediate attention. Would seven-thirty be too early?"

"Damn right, it would. I'll be in about ten."

She smiled. "I'll try to have a draft of our partnership agreement ready . . . that is if you haven't changed your mind."

"No, but I'm warning you . . . the partnership isn't going to make me change my ways."

"Nor do I expect to change mine," she said. "Goodnight, Josh." Having dismissed him, she hurried up the stairs and disappeared into the hallway at the top.

He was left with no doubt in his mind that she had meant what she had said when she announced that their relationship would be confined to a business one. That was her pronouncement, though, not his. Agreements could be renegotiated, and he thought of himself as a persuasive negotiator.

For a moment, Josh considered going up to his own room. If he had any sense, he would take advantage of the soft bed while he had a chance. The bed was luring him but sleeping alone in it was not so enticing. There were too many thoughts buzzing in his head this night: the plans for Erin McKenna's ransom; the new law partnership; his undefined feelings for Danna Sinclair; his need for a woman's touch. All that his bed offered him now was a night of restless tossing.

He left the Exchange and walked out onto the dark street. He strolled aimlessly for most of an hour, crisscrossing the plaza to the Hidalgo hacienda.

This time luck was with him. When the door opened, he was

greeted by the young maid, Rosa, who stared at him wide-eyed and hesitant. "I came to see Constanza," Josh said. "Is she home this evening?"

The girl fidgeted and tossed a nervous look over her shoulder. "*Si*, señor. But I am sorry to say she cannot see you. Her family is at the *ranchero* this week. And . . . and . . . " Tears welled up in the Mexican girl's big eyes.

"It is alright, Rosa," The familiar voice came from behind her. "I will speak with señor Rivers."

"But señorita," the girl protested. "Señor Hidalgo said—"

"I know what he said, Rosa," said Constanza, as she came up beside her. "You know also you will not speak a single word of señor Rivers's visit here or you will no longer be employed in this household. Do you understand?"

"*Si,* señorita," she whispered meekly and stepped away.

"I've had better welcomes," Josh said as he faced the dark-eyed beauty standing in the doorway, wearing a white, cotton dress that left her shoulders bare and revealed a generous portion of her full, round breasts. The thin line of her lips and the firm set of her jaw said she was angry at him, that he was an unwelcome intruder. The dark limpid pools of her eyes said that she shared his hunger.

"My father has ordered that I not see you anymore." Her voice was husky, unsure.

"Would you prefer I leave?"

"We should talk. You may come in."

She led him through the foyer and into a small sitting room that was decorated with woven Mexican rugs, Indian pottery, and paintings representative of both cultures. It was a cozy room furnished with cushioned chairs and a stuffed leather-covered couch that faced a large, adobe fireplace wherein orange-red flames danced to the snapping and crackling of burning mountain pine. A bearskin rug in front of the fireplace added to the feeling of warmth, and as Josh sat down on the couch, he welcomed the warm breath of the fire that chased away the chill of the night air. He noted that Constanza placed herself at the opposite end of the couch, safely out of his reach. Now she sat there staring at him with the same severe look frozen on her face.

"Well, you might as well spit it out," he said.

"What do you mean?"

"Tell me why I am suddenly treated like smallpox around the Hidalgo hacienda."

"It is my father. I have fought him on this, but after today, I'm not so certain."

"I thought your father and I were on fairly good terms, considering I am a gringo and a lawyer. I was never sure which was the worse evil."

Her eyes flashed. "You are being unfair to my father. He has always welcomed you into our home. Can you say he has not been a gracious host?"

"No, I can't." He was more subdued now. "I apologize if I suggested otherwise. But why the sudden hostility on your father's part?"

Her eyes were downcast, a rarity for Constanza, who was ordinarily proud, defiant. "It is not you, so much as it is certain plans my father has."

"What kind of plans?"

"He is arranging a marriage."

"Marriage? For you?"

She looked up in tear-glazed eyes. "But who else? I am his only child. A daughter. Such things are arranged among my people. A custom."

Josh snapped. "Not by law. New Mexico is a territory of the United States. You don't have to marry anyone you don't want to. Who is this prospective bridegroom anyway? What kind of a man would want his woman this way?"

"He is a very prominent citizen of our territory. My father says he will be very powerful someday. His name is Andrew Robinson. Judge Andrew Robinson."

"Robinson! He's twice your age."

"Yes, but he is still a relatively young man. And quite handsome in a distinguished sort of way. He has been calling at our home for a month now."

"Ever since I left," Josh interjected sarcastically.

"Yes, that is true. And he has been a perfect gentleman, and I do not find him repulsive. He says our marriage would be a perfect political union. A pure descendant of Spain with an American aristocrat. My father agrees. He says Judge Robinson has important family ties to banking interests in New York and Massachusetts."

"So that's what it comes down to. Like all other ranchers in the territory, Miguel Hidalgo is pressed for cash."

"Many of our mines have been closed down because of Apache troubles," Constanza said matter-of-factly.

"So Miguel mortgages his daughter."

"I will not permit you to speak in such a disrespectful way about my father."

Josh sighed. "Again I apologize. You aren't going to tell me you are in love with Andrew Robinson."

"No, but my mother says that will come later. She is very much in love with my father, but the first time she met him was the day before their wedding. It was all arranged and it has worked out very well."

"But you are not your mother."

They sat in silence for some moments, staring at the flickering flames of fire. Josh could not believe what he had heard. Constanza. She had always had a mind of her own. He knew that Spanish families had strong family bonds, but he could not see Constanza bending to her father's will on something so important and personal as marriage. And to Andrew Robinson, to boot. It was beginning to look like the courtroom was not the only battlefield upon which he would have to face Robinson. As he thought about it, though, it occurred to him that Robinson had the best of it in both instances. Judge Andrew Robinson would declare his own winner in the courtroom. Suitor Andrew Robinson would win Constanza's hand because Josh was not ready to fight for it.

"I can't feel anything but sadness about all this, Constanza," Josh said softly. "You're too much woman to have such a decision made for you by your father."

"But I love my father. I was not sure of this until today, but now I am, and I see it as something I can do for him and for my family. And it is time for me to marry. I have had no other proposals."

"You said you were not sure about your father's decision until today. What happened?"

"My father said your intentions about me were not serious. I did not believe him. Then I heard of the woman who returned with you. It is said she walked nearly naked into Andrew's courtroom. I was told you had been on the trail with her many days. Under the circumstances, I would find it very hard to believe that you did not have your way with her."

Josh could not say who had her or his way with whom, but it was clear that Judge Robinson had wasted no time passing the word to Constanza.

"I must know, Josh. Did you make love to this woman?"

"If I had, I wouldn't tell you. That's a question I would not answer about any woman. I have never asked you about any other men. I have no right to." He moved closer to her and reached out and took her hand. Her palm was warm and slick with perspiration. "Constanza, you've been precious to me these past months, and I want you to know that you were the only woman to make me think about marriage again. I have loved you. I still do. In a very special way, I guess. I've asked myself time and again, is it a marrying kind of love? It is damned close, but if it were in fact, I don't know if I'd have to ask the question. I know this, I can't ask you to marry me now, and I can't promise you that I ever would. But you'll always be dear to me. If you're convinced you can find happiness with Andrew Robinson, I wish you the best."

Her full red lips began to quiver and tiny tears squeezed out the corners of her eyes and began to trickle down her cheeks. Suddenly, she threw herself into his arms and buried her face into his chest as he wrapped his arms around her. She started to sob uncontrollably, her body shaking violently. He caressed her back and bare shoulders gently, trying to sooth her pain, yet knowing he could not reach it.

"Connie," he said softly, "don't be a fool. You're too much woman to martyr yourself to your father or to any man. Don't waste your life with a man you don't love."

She raised her head, pulling slightly back from him. In a whispered voice that seemed to break free from her gasps for breath, she said, "I have already wasted too much of my life on a man I do love."

Josh wagged his head. "No, Connie, don't ever believe that. Loving someone, being loved, is never wasted no matter how short a time. It's a banquet, a feast, and there are too many people starving for it." His face moved down to hers and her lips parted slightly to receive his own.

Suddenly, it was as if the hot heat of the coals in the fireplace had transferred itself to them, for they were both caught up in the raging fire that could only burn itself out. Clinging together, they dropped from the couch to the plush fur of the bearskin rug. Almost frantically, they groped and unbuttoned and tugged at each other's garments, each helping the other to wriggle free of their cumbersome clothes. When they were naked, they attacked each other like two mountain cats that were at once playful and fierce. Her teeth dug into his thighs, and her fingers became claws that raked his back and chest and shoulders. He pinned her to the floor, and they probed with their tongues, explored with their fingers, as if embarked on an adventure that was virgin to them both.

There were no words between them, only moans and purrs and groans and gasps. And finally, when he drove himself into her, she bucked beneath him like a wild mare turned loose from the catch pen, and he rode her like a rider that could not be thrown, until long, deep spasms shook his loins and she milked him nearly empty before her entire body shuddered again and again, and he felt her legs quivering against his thighs.

They lay silently in each other's arms for some minutes before they coupled again. This time, tenderly, almost lazily, and afterward, it was over. Constanza slipped away from Josh and without a word began dressing. He took his cue and began to gather up his own things.

When they were both dressed, he followed her to the door. As they paused there in the open doorway, Josh looked down at an impassive face that was not even betrayed by the dull eyes that had gone from sparkling obsidian to dead coals.

"Please do not come here again, Joshua," she said coldly as she stepped inside and pushed the door shut behind her.

28

"HOW MUCH LONGER do we wait?" Cal asked as he downed the last of the sourdough biscuits. "They're two days late."

Josh, stretched out on his bedroll near the dying embers of their campfire, clasped his hands behind his head and stared at the star-spangled sky above. He sorted out the Big Dipper and from its bearings got a fix on the North Star. Finally he answered his brother, "At least two more. The attack at Palo Duro probably scattered the Kwahadi to hell and gone. It could be taking some time to regroup. Or with the soldiers in the field, they might have had to change their route."

"Yeah," Cal said, "or Quanah Parker could be dead. Or the McKenna girl. Or he could have just plain changed his mind. A thousand things could have gone wrong, any one of which could cause us to get our scalps lifted if we stay here too goddamn long. Damn it, Josh, if a Comanche war party shows up, they can squash us like a couple of piss ants and help themselves to three hundred gold double eagles. There won't be a damn thing we can do about it."

"If the Comanche take a notion to help themselves, they'll

take them. It's as simple as that."

"What about our scalps?"

"You can leave if you want. You're not hogtied here."

"Shit, I didn't say I was wanting to leave. I've never met Quanah Parker face to face. I wouldn't miss this party."

"Then quit your belly aching."

"Damn you, Josh, you've had something working on you ever since we rode out of Santa Fe. You've been like you had a cactus spine up your ass. I might expect that from Ham, but you usually aren't that hard to ride fence line with." Josh said nothing. "You know, I have it figured that you're acting like a man with woman troubles. Is that it? Is it that Texas tornado you took on in your office?" He went on without waiting for a reply. "Damn, I never thought of it. Jessica. You were with her all that time, and then I stepped in."

"No, it's not Jessica," Josh snapped, "and the only problem I got right now is getting Erin McKenna back to Santa Fe."

"Well, I'm sure glad it doesn't have anything to do with Jessica. I've got to say I'm more than a little smitten by that gal. Did you know she wants to open up a theater in Santa Fe? Do you think folks there are ready for that?"

"They'd damn well better be because Jessica Chandler's likely to make it happen."

"She's looking for investors. She's planning to talk to you about how to set up the business end of it."

"It sounds like an intriguing investment," Josh said. "It might be something I'd be interested in being a part of. You might consider it yourself."

"I'm past the considering stage, big brother. I already committed myself to a tenth share. Two hundred dollars . . . about everything I've got put away."

A mournful howling followed by a frenzied yipping that echoed through the canyon walls to the north interrupted their conversation. Josh tensed and raised himself up on his elbow, listening intently as some of the horses whinnied nervously. "That's strange," Josh said. "I didn't hear a single coyote last night."

"You aren't hearing one tonight, either," Cal said softly, a ragged edge in his voice. "Those are Comanche you're hearing. My guess is they're checking us out . . . being certain we didn't bring some friends. The question is whether they're your Kwahadi friends or some other renegades that just happened along. I suspect we'll find out soon enough. Any ideas?"

"Just sit and wait, I guess. They know where we're at. We haven't made any effort to hide it." He tossed a weary look toward the cottonwoods that surrounded the little clearing where they'd set up camp. "There's likely more of them within spitting distance."

"They'll make themselves known in due time." Cal dug into his rawhide possibles bag and retrieved a well-used corncob pipe. He stuffed some of the contents of his tobacco pouch into the charred pipe bowl and ignited a twig on the blinking red cinders of their campfire and lit it. He leaned back against a tree stump and began to smoke leisurely, as if savoring the balmy night air the final few minutes before he turned in.

Josh lay back on his bedroll and seemingly returned to his scrutiny of the sky. They waited without speaking, listening to the Comanche-coyotes raise their ruckus in the canyon. But Josh's calm, almost serene manner, was belied by the twisting and churning of his gut, a relentless pounding in his skull.

How many times had he seen death? Faced it? Somehow it had never gotten any easier, and he was struck by a heightened awareness of the fragility of human life.

Abruptly, the howling and barking stopped, and the night was still. Josh could hear a beetle crawling through the grass next to his blanket. It was as if the moment had been orchestrated for effect by the supreme conductor in the sky.

"You are very brave, word bearer." The familiar lyrical voice came from the dense grove of trees behind Cal.

Josh sat up as She Who Speaks walked into the clearing. Cal continued to puff on his pipe and turned only slightly as she moved past him and around the fire toward Josh on the other side. Josh stood up to face her as she came close enough to touch. She was dressed in deerskin britches and a painted war shirt more common to the Comanche warrior. One side of her face was painted with alternate stripes: white and black. It gave her a ghostly appearance yet somehow made her beauty more exotic. When their eyes met, though, Josh saw pain there he had not seen before. Then he realized her face was drawn and a bit haggard.

"It is a very thin line between bravery and foolishness," Josh said. "I have never been sure where one ended and the other began."

"I think you are more certain than you say." She nodded almost imperceptibly toward Cal who still had not moved from his tree stump backrest. "The other white man? He can be trusted?"

"He is my brother. He can be trusted."

She showed no further interest in Cal. "You have kept your promise, word bearer."

"Yes, I have. I assume Quanah will keep his."

She did not reply directly. "We must talk." She let herself down on Josh's bedroll, sitting there cross legged and signaling that he should join her. When he was settled on the blanket, she spoke. "I am to ask if you have inquired about terms for peace. Have you started your work as Quanah's lawyer?"

"Yes, I have. I have sent word to a friend of my father's at Fort Bliss. He is a very influential man in our government. His word is good. He will make contacts discreetly. After I have taken the McKenna girl back to Santa Fe and finished some business there, I will ride to Fort Bliss to meet with him. I will try to learn what the best is that we can expect to accomplish. But tell me, how can I get word to Quanah?"

"When you have something to say, return to this place. You will be found."

"I'm not sure I like your way of making contact."

"It must be this way. No harm will come to you in this place." She unfastened a deerskin pouch that had been tied to her waist and handed it to Josh. "I am to give you this. It is a payment toward your fees you will charge for your services to our people."

Josh shook his head in disbelief as he opened the pouch. "A retainer from Quanah Parker," he said, "who would believe it?" He poured part of the contents into the palm of his hand: gold nuggets. "My God, if these are as good as I think they are, there must be a thousand dollars worth in this pouch. I don't think Quanah realizes what he has given me here. I don't need all of this to start work."

"Quanah knows more than you think. He wants you to understand the urgency of our cause. With this, there should be no question that you can devote the proper efforts to representing the Kwahadi."

"That's true. Quanah or She Who Speaks has an exceptionally keen insight to how things work in the white man's world. I have a business partner who will look after our other clients. Your case will have first priority on my time." He paused. "After I have taken Erin McKenna home. Tell me, She Who Speaks, Erin is here? There is no problem?"

"She is here. There is no problem. It proved easier than it might have. Her husband was killed, as was mine, when the soldiers attacked the village. She is with child and her health is not robust. Since no man claims her, Quanah, as war chief, will release her to you. In an earlier time, the woman would have stayed with the People to bring another child to the band. Quanah says it does not matter now. We shall all be white soon."

"I'm sorry for the loss of your husband."

She cast her head downward momentarily. "He died a warrior's death facing the pony soldiers while his family escaped. There is no greater honor."

"I suppose I am pushing my luck, but I must ask you this, She Who Speaks. My own son, can you tell me anything? I will return this gold for my own son. I'll be The People's lawyer without fees."

"I can tell you little. Quanah is trying to learn of your son. You must understand that there are many bands of The People. Your son is not in our village, but Quanah will do what he can. He promises this."

Her promise was evasive, but there was firmness in her eyes that told him it was useless to pursue the matter. His hopes had been revived. As the word bearer, he would have other opportunities to track down his lost son or to learn what his fate had been.

"Now," She Who Speaks said, "we must talk of the terms."

And they did, for the better part of an hour. She Who Speaks presented Quanah's demands, explained to Josh the chief's goals, outlined the blue-eyed Comanche's vision of the future and set forth what was negotiable and what was not.

When they neared the end of their discussion, Josh found himself in awe of Quanah Parker's sophistication, his insight into the human mind and a way of life that was all but foreign to him. And he gained an even greater respect for the brilliant mind of the young woman who spoke for the Kwahadi chief.

Finally, she rose from the ground and asked, "The gold dollars?"

Josh got up and lifted his saddle, which was near the bedroll, and revealed several leather bags beneath it. "These are called double eagles . . . twenty-dollar gold pieces. Three hundred of them."

She raised her hand toward the sky, and a Comanche warrior appeared from the trees and quickly retrieved the treasure.

Suddenly, She Who Speaks, without a word, disappeared into the brush. Josh guessed she had declared their meeting adjourned. He and Cal rose and Josh looked over at his brother, who simply shrugged.

Momentarily, a young woman with an immensely swollen belly emerged from the darkness and stood near the fading embers of their fire, her eyes wide and fearful. Erin McKenna had arrived for her journey home.

29

IT HAD BEEN slow going. Erin McKenna was obviously a good rider, which was not surprising given that she had grown up on a ranch. They had brought a string of half dozen horses along, thinking they might have to switch off to make time on the return trip to Santa Fe. But the young woman's health had obviously not thrived during her captivity, and carrying a child in her belly had not made the journey any easier.

Erin had retreated into a refuge of silence when she was abandoned by the Comanche at the campsite. She seemed angry about her circumstances and responded to directions, but her vocabulary seemed limited to "yes" and "no." Josh and Cal had tacitly agreed they would not press her for conversation at this point. The rough-hewn Cal, however, had been surprisingly attentive to the young lady's needs, seeing that she drank enough water and calling for rest breaks more frequently than Josh would have preferred.

At the rate they were moving, Josh calculated they were about a week from Santa Fe, and it was ten days before the continued hearing, so if there were no surprises they should arrive with time to spare. With an ailing, pregnant woman in tow, they could not be assured there would be no surprises.

Cal called to him from behind, where he had been riding with Erin. "Josh, pull up." He trotted his big bay gelding up next to Josh.

"She's not doing so good, Josh," Cal said. "She can barely stay on her horse. I asked her if she was hurting, but she didn't answer."

Josh looked back and saw that Erin was swaying in her saddle. He had hoped for a few more hours of travel time, but she wasn't going to make it. He surveyed the terrain for a likely campsite. They'd tried to stay within an easy ride from what Cal said was Thirsty Man's Creek, which rarely ran dry, even in late August. The creek trickled out of eastern New Mexico and gathered strength as it sliced across west Texas before it emptied into the Red River to the east. His eyes picked up several clumps of trees. This signaled an oasis of sorts in the middle of the dry, rocky Texas prairie.

He pointed in that direction. "Cal," he said, "over there." He turned to his brother and was taken aback when he saw Erin McKenna cradled in Cal's arms, her head nested in his chest. The big man reined his horse forward, Erin's mare tagging along behind.

"She started sliding out of the saddle," Cal said, "and I picked her off the mare. Poor thing's done in. Tougher than a boot, but she's reached her limit."

"Well, let's set up camp and see what we can do about it."

30

THIRSTY MAN'S CREEK ran clear and raced powerfully over its rocky bed at this spot. Scrub willows and healthy patches of buffalo grass fringed the banks, offering welcome shade and pasturage for the horses. Josh staked out the horses while Cal tried to make Erin comfortable on some blankets.

He had retrieved some water in a canvas basin from the creek and now was bathing the young woman's face with a wet rag torn from his shirt.

Her eyelids fluttered open, and she looked at him with confused eyes. "What happened?"

"You passed out. We decided to stop here for the night and catch some rest."

"I'm sorry. I'm slowing you down, and I haven't been very pleasant, have I?"

He evaded a direct response. "It's nice to hear you speak. I've been worried about you."

"You've gone out of your way to be kind to me. Daddy never put up with my black moods. You shouldn't either."

He smiled at her. "You've been through a lot. You're entitled to a black mood, I think."

She returned a faint smile, and he suddenly realized how pretty this copper-haired woman with the dusting of freckles across her nose and below her eyes was. She was sweaty and dirt-caked and bloated with child but could still catch a man's eye.

Erin winced noticeably and took a deep breath.

"What is it?" Cal asked.

"I'm not sure. The baby, I think."

"Just moving, I assume?"

She shifted and emitted a soft moan. "More than that, I think."

A wave of panic swept through him. "You're not talking about the baby coming?"

"I am."

"You can't. Not here. Not now."

"I can."

"What can I do?"

"Get the Dutch oven from the packhorse and boil some water. That'll get you out of the way till you're needed. We'll want a small blanket. Do you have an extra you can cut in half?"

"Yes ma'am."

"Everybody back home calls me 'Erin' That would do fine."

"Yes, ma'am." He got up and started looking for the Dutch oven, which Josh had unloaded before he staked out the horses. Then he saw Josh walking toward him from downstream.

"Everything alright? You look sick," Josh said.

"We're having a baby."

"Well, yes, Miss McKenna's having a baby . . . eventually."

"Not eventually . . . now."

"Oh shit."

"Do something."

"Why me?"

"I'm doing the water."

Josh brushed past him and Cal followed. Josh knelt down next to Erin. "How do you feel?"

"Pardon me for saying so, but that's kind of a dumb question."

"Do you know how to go about this? Ever helped birth a baby?"

"I helped with some Comanche babies. Not that much different than cows. But I don't know if I'll be as brave as a Comanche squaw about it."

Cal interjected, "Can you tell us what to do?"

"More or less." She sighed heavily. "The pains are coming pretty fast. Help me get my britches off."

Cal helped her out of the baggy buckskin britches that had been tied loosely about her waist, while Josh turned his attention to preparing the water. She wore no undergarments, and Cal was mildly embarrassed by her nakedness, more so when a blast of water squirted from between her thighs. "Oh God," he whispered.

"Oh Jesus," she said, "It hurts, but I can't stop it. I'm pushing hard. It's coming. Get ready."

"Get ready for what?"

"To take the baby, damn it."

Cal could hardly stand to see her in pain like this, huffing and groaning. Thankfully, Josh returned with the water and blankets.

Suddenly, a round bulge covered with black, matted fuzz emerged from Erin's vagina, and instinctively, Cal's big hands moved to meet the baby. Erin gave a final push, and a wet, slippery, bloody baby slid into his waiting hands. "Oh, my God." The baby started to cry, and Cal almost dropped it.

"What is it?" Erin asked, her voice weak.

"A baby."

"Cal, don't be an idiot," Josh said. "Boy or girl?"

Cal looked down, studying the red, wrinkled creature in is hands. "I don't see any boy parts. I guess it's a girl. She's beautiful." He guessed that was what he was supposed to say, but he always thought babies were kind of ugly.

Erin said, "Josh, you need to cut the cord. Clean your hunting knife in the hot water, and then cut the cord about six inches out from the baby." Josh obeyed.

"What do I do with her?" Cal asked.

"Bring her to me. You can help me clean her up and wrap her in a blanket. It will be dark soon, so I'll need to move closer to the fire with her."

Several hours later, the baby girl was suckling at her mother's breast. When she had drunk her fill, she dropped off to sleep. Cal had not left Erin's side for more than a few moments at a time, and when the new mother started to fade away, he took the baby from her arms and held her in his own until it was time for the newborn to eat again.

Cal saw his brother watching him from the other side of the fire, as he cuddled the baby. "You're wanting to say something . . . spit it out."

"Nothing. Just having trouble thinking of you as a midwife, that's all. You did good, little brother."

31

CAL WORRIED ABOUT Erin. They were two days out from Santa Fe, and he could see she was fading from exhaustion. The baby thrived, and for the most part, slept as they rode, evidently liking the rocking motion of the horse. She rode with Cal most of the time, nestled in a sling he had fashioned from blanket fragments and slipped over his neck. He liked the feel of her pressed against his chest, and he was glad he could relieve some of the burden from Erin and allow her to doze in the saddle between feedings.

They would be stopping early again. They had made surprisingly good time, thanks to Erin's perseverance. They had held over a day at the birthing place, and he could not imagine the pain horseback must be causing her private area, but she had not complained once. Of course, he supposed that might not be something a lady would want to talk about.

Since the night of the baby's birth, Cal had rarely left her side. He had quietly rolled out his blankets next to hers and chastely spent the nights at her side, while the baby snuggled near her mother's breast. Erin seemed to accept it as the natural order of things. The baby did not have a name yet, and Cal had pointed it out this morning. "Tonight," Erin said, "we'll give her a name."

That evening they had set up camp at the broken remains of what had once been an adobe house. Two partial walls cornered and formed a natural shelter for the visitors, but Josh had opted to sleep out on the open prairie some hundred feet distant and had departed as soon as they finished cleaning up after supper. Cal wasn't certain whether his brother was affording him some sort of unnecessary privacy or just escaping the sleep-interrupting cries of a hungry baby.

Cal and Erin leaned back against an adobe wall as the baby slept between them. It was not yet eight o'clock, but Cal guessed Erin would drop off to sleep soon.

"I said we'd name the baby tonight," Erin said. "It's time." Without thinking, Cal reached over and took her hand. He had fallen into the habit since the night of the baby's birth.

"Well, what have you decided?"

"That you should name the baby."

"Me? Why me?"

"You were the first to hold her. And I don't have any inspiration."

"I *have* been thinking about it. What about 'Willow'? She was born on a creek bank near a lot of willows. It could be a Comanche name or an American name, so it honors her dual heritage."

"Her father was a brave warrior, a good man. I hated him at first, but I became fond of him. He died saving our lives. I like the idea that her name comes from the prairie. Yes, I think 'Willow' suits her fine."

"Well, now we've settled that. What happens next for you? We'll be in Santa Fe after one more night on the trail, and we'll meet the judge's deadline by a few days."

"I've been thinking about it, but I'm a little scared. I guess whenever the legal stuff gets untangled, I'll own a ranch. I think I want to go back there. It's home, and I'd like the . . . Willow to grow up there. Besides, right now I crave the privacy of the ranch . . . where people can't gossip about me for having a child with a Comanche warrior or ridicule my half-breed daughter."

"You're worrying too much. The melting pot is alive and well in the Southwest. Three-fourths of the people in this territory have Indian blood. And mark my word, someday Willow will be proud as heck of her Comanche ancestors."

"I hope you're right. But I don't know anything about running a ranch, and I don't know what's happened to the cow herd while I've been gone. Most of the cattle have probably wandered off or been rustled."

"My father's got a young German cowhand who has great potential as a foreman. I could get the okay from Dad to hire him for your ranch. And, if you'd let me, I'd go with you and help you get settled in and round up your herd."

"You would? I'd be forever grateful."

"Consider it done."

She squeezed his hand. "You're a good man. This gives me so much peace of mind." She slid down onto her blankets, and in only a few minutes, he could hear the rhythmic breathing of deep sleep.

32

JOSH AND DANNA were seated at a small conference table in the Rivers and Sinclair library. Danna thought he was a little full of himself over his success on the Staked Plains, but she decided he was entitled. His retrieval of Erin McKenna had won her case. Upon presenting Erin in Judge Robinson's court this morning, he had promptly made his determination of heirship in favor of the deceased's daughter.

Danna had advised Erin she would most certainly be successful in pursuing an application to remove her uncle as administrator of the estate and appointing someone of her choosing. As expected, she authorized Danna to proceed. To the lawyer's surprise, though, she asked that Calvin Rivers be appointed as her uncle's successor.

"I thought this was a partner's conference," Josh said. "You seem to be someplace else."

"Sorry. First, I want to congratulate you on your successful trip. This was one of those cases where the facts were more important than lawyering, and you drug the evidence in from the hands of the Comanche. And eventually we'll see some good fees from this case."

"I've got to give Cal most of the credit. I don't know if I'd have got the young lady back on my own. From the beginning he adopted her like a mother cat taking on a stray kitten, and then he took over care of the baby, too. I absolutely couldn't believe what I was seeing."

Danna couldn't believe it, either. She knew the man had a good heart, but she didn't see a sign of domesticity during her brief and passionate relationship with him. She had realized quickly that they were not destined for the long term.

"And he's going back to the ranch with her," Josh said. "I suppose his enchantment with Erin and Willow will wear out eventually, but who am I to say?"

Getting back to business, Danna said, "The office is doing well. I've been working night and day, but I love it. I can tell you it beats waiting for another client to come in the door. I can tell that a few clients are uneasy about a woman taking on their work, but in the end they just want things done."

"Speaking of clients, I haven't had a chance to tell you about a new one."

"I'm listening."

"Quanah Parker."

She was incredulous. "You're serious?"

Josh plucked a little rawhide bag from his coat pocket and dumped the contents on the table. "Our retainer."

"I assume those are gold nuggets?"

"Yes. I'll take them to the assayer to see what they're worth . . . maybe exchange them for coinage."

"Given your history with the Comanche, I'm very surprised. What did you agree to do for this?"

Josh outlined his peace negotiation mission. When he finished, he added, "I also have a very personal reason for taking this on. In the course of my work, I will have many opportunities to meet with the Comanche and Quanah. I'm convinced that this will enable me to eventually lead to learning Michael's fate, for better or worse."

"I understand. So you'll be hitting the trails again soon?"

"Within the next few days. I guess I did need a partner. You seem to have everything under control in the office."

"I'm trying, and I'd like your agreement to employ an associate if I should find a qualified prospect. I have a hunch you're never going to spend much time in this office . . . and I won't object if you're going to harvest retainers like you've dropped on the table. But we need to be able to turn out the work if we're going to grow the firm, and I can't carry the workload myself over the long haul."

Josh turned silent, and she was convinced he was preparing his counter-argument to her proposal. Finally, he spoke. "Look, lady law wrangler, I don't want to worry about all of this office crap. Do what you think best. I hereby ordain you managing partner of The Law Firm of Rivers and Sinclair."

About the Author

Ron Schwab is the author of *Sioux Sunrise, Paint the Hills Red, Medicine Wheel, Night of the Coyote*, and *Last Will*, the latter two of which were nominated for Best Novel Peacemaker Awards by Western Fictioneers. He is a member of the Western Writers of America, Western Fictioneers, and Mystery Writers of America.

Ron and his wife, Bev, divide their time between their home in Fairbury, Nebraska and their cabin in the Kansas Flint Hills.

To learn more about Ron and his books, please visit www.RonSchwabBooks.com.

Made in United States
Troutdale, OR
07/20/2023

11448026R00137